The Bold and the Ugly Truth

Hannah D. Spivey

The Bold and the Ugly Truth

Acknowledgement

First, I'd like to thank God for instilling so much strength in me to do what I have to do and want to do. He's been the greatest source in my life and I have him nothing but the glory. I dedicate this book to the late great Adrienne Strachn, who be-lieved in me and called me a New York Times Bestselling Author. She saw more in me than I could imagine and I thank her wholly for that. R.I.P, Adrienne. You are no longer with us but you'll NEVER be forgotten. I also like to thank my editor and sister friend Aquila Butler, Rashida Forbes and Jason Yates who posed for the book cover, and Marco who is the owner of Visual Noise Photography.

To my grandmother and other cheerleader, Bertha Johnson. Thank you so much for your unwavering support and unconditional love. To my sister, Naomi Spivey - you and I have had our ups and downs but our bond is unbreakable. I love you, sis. To my mother and father, Annette and Nelvin Spivey - we don't always understand each other but I will always love both of you unconditionally. To my wonderful friends and associates, Jesse Perry, Nasi, Rowe, and Atarah Eleazar, Jakeem Smith, Kim Underwood, Gary Burton, Nicole Hodges, Joyce Badie, Latoya Neal, Keturah, Marisa Johnson, Veronica Cudger, Angel

Jennings, Kirstin Reid, Shirley Greg, Priscilla Manet, and most of all my recently departed sister friend, Lisa Harris. I thank you all so much for being great aspects in my life. Lisa, I wish you wouldn't have left us so soon. May you R.I.P (Rest in Paradise). Again, thank you all and the best is yet to come! *Smiling*

The Bold and the Ugly Truth

Chapter 1.

In Jesus' Name, Amen

Samuel looked straight into the multiple camera lenses; his posture was straight as he stared into the eyes of America. He looked rather distinguished in his navy blue pinstripe suit. His processed hair was sleek like Duke Ellington's, and his stony facial expression gave him a masked look. As soon as he opened his mouth, you would've thought Billy Dee Williams had died and reincarnated himself inside of him. Samuel sounded precisely like him—cool, calm, and collected. When he spoke, it was as if the whole atmosphere came to a standstill.

"To all the soldiers in the Middle East, I'm going to pray for your safe return. I take my hat off to all of you for selflessly defending our beautiful nation. My heart also goes out to the families of the soldiers who lost their lives in the line of duty. I want to take this God sent opportunity to praise our father. Let us all pray." Samuel closed his eyes and he put both of his hands together.

"Dear Lord, I ask if you can lay your hands on the brave soldiers who are risking their lives for this wonderful nation. I ask if you can bring every last one of them back home in one piece so that they can reunite with their loved ones. As for those who weren't fortunate enough to survive, I know it was in your will. They are now in your hands and they will forever live on through their families. You are the reason for the season and I love you more than I love myself. I will lay my life down for you. In Jesus' name…Amen."

"Amen," the congregation repeated in unison.

Samuel finally opened his eyes. His prayers were always powerful and heartfelt. His members always commended him for his epic sermons, but they had no clue that his prayers and sermons weren't genuine. If they'd been mind readers, they would have been shocked by the thoughts that were jumping around in his head. Because all the while he was thinking, Christianity really makes my balls itch!

Chapter 2

Overbearing Father

Samuel was glad to finally be home. He sat in his La-Z-Boy and he removed his shoes; he was pooped. I sure could use a can of Miller Light, he thought. Samuel hadn't consumed alcohol since he'd taken the pastoral oath at the World Faith Missionary Baptist Church nine years ago. He released a frustrated sigh. His wife Pauline was in the kitchen preparing supper while his daughter Chastity was upstairs watching, That's So Raven. By this time, he was normally in his office working on his sermon, but he didn't feel like doing anything that night. All he wanted to do was get his mind off church, eat dinner, watch a movie, make love to his wife, and call it a night.

He was flipping through the channels until he saw the infamous Pastor Kerney Thomas acting like a world class fool. Pastor Thomas' sermons were so devised and comical, he could have won a Tony award for "Best Fraudulent Pastor." The way Pastor Thomas was whooping and hollering, the congregation must have been witless for taking him seriously.

This nigga is a fool ass clown, but he's funny as hell, Samuel thought.

He felt a laugh coming on because the pastor's performance wasn't going to allow him to sit in his La-Z-Boy without laughing his head off. As soon as Pastor Thomas screamed, "Gawwwwddd!" Samuel almost fell out of his seat. He was laughing so hard, he nearly choked on his tongue. His laughter and coughing alarmed Pauline, and she quickly stormed into the living room to see what was going on.

"Are you okay, sweetie?" she asked.

Samuel continued to laugh for a minute, then finally sat up and cleared his throat. "Yes, baby. Everything is fine. I'm just laughing at this silly pastor on television."

Pauline screwed up her face as if she'd caught Samuel watching pornography. "Lord, have mercy. What on earth are you doing watching that no-good clown preacher? The network should pull the plug on his ministry. He's got a lot of nerve behaving the way he does. I ought to call that network and complain about his so-called ministry. He ought to be ashamed of himself. The Lord is going to strike the fakeness out of him," she huffed. Whenever Pauline got upset, her nose would turn red like a beet.

"I couldn't agree with you more baby, but I give the man props for being a good comedian," Samuel replied and laughed again.

Pauline wasn't the least bit amused. She walked over to the television and turned it off.

"What did you do that for?!" he complained. What he was thinking was, Bitch, have you lost your damn mind? But he didn't want to incite an argument.auline was two months pregnant with their second child and the last thing he wanted to do was upset her.

"Samuel Lee Baker, you are a man of the cloth. Watching other pastors mock the Lord is just wrong. You're a best-selling author with over 40,000 church minions and a seven-year-old daughter. You should be setting a better example than this. What do you have to say for yourself?" Pauline angrily asked and folded her arms.

Samuel loved when Pauline frowned. It made her look even more stunning. Whenever she got mad, she would wiggle her sharp nose and poke out her pouty lips. She stood at five feet, nine inches tall with a butterscotch complexion, full pouty lips, and striking yellow-brown eyes. People constantly remarked to her that she looked like Jada Pinkett-Smith and Kerry Washington. Samuel felt his shaft rise like a biscuit.

Her sexy frown was turning him on. He stared at her and remained silent. She was very familiar with that seductive look.

"Oh no, mister! You aren't getting off the hook that easily. Undressing me with your eyes isn't going to work this time." Samuel continued ignoring her and approached her. "Samuel, I'm serious." Pauline tried to muster up the most serious face as possible but it didn't work.

Samuel slowly walked toward her and finally said, "I know baby, and I'm sorry." His Billy Dee Williams-like voice was enough to give her goose nipples.

"Samuel, I'm not playing with you." Pauline was finding it difficult to resist a smile.

"You look so sexy when you pout," he said. He wrapped his strong arms around her waist and began showering her with kisses. He started kissing on her neck and nibbling on her right earlobe. She released a moan and forgot about the way she'd scolded him just moments earlier for watching Pastor Thomas Kerney. The scent of Samuel's cologne was intoxicating. She and Samuel could have embraced each other all night long in that same spot without moving. They stared into each other's eyes and began kissing. Samuel parted her lips with his tongue. He picked her up and was about to carry her upstairs when he heard the doorbell ring.

Ain't this about a son of a bitch? he thought.

Whoever it was ringing his door after 7 pm had better have a good damn excuse for derailing his lovemaking plans. Samuel wanted to cuss out whoever the uninvited visitor was, but he also wanted to ignore the visitor. However, the determined visitor rang the doorbell three more consecutive times.

"Sweetie, let me go see who it is," Pauline said.

"Come on, baby. I'm sure it's probably one of the girl scouts again," Samuel protested.

"What if it's something important, Samuel? It could be a life or death situation."

Samuel sucked his teeth and finally put Pauline down.

Pauline walked to the door to see who it was. "Who is it?" she asked.

"It's Woodrow; open up the door!" the deep voice demanded.

"Just a minute, Papa Woodrow!" she replied.

Woodrow was Samuel's overly religious father. He was a proud and righteous man. You see, Woodrow was a God-fearing perfectionist who lived vicariously through the Bible, and no matter how hard Samuel tried to please him, it just wasn't sufficient enough.

"It's your daddy," Pauline turned to Samuel and whispered.

"Well, don't just stand there. Let him in!" Samuel hissed. He wasn't necessarily hissing at Pauline. He was really mad at his father for inflicting himself upon him and his family at an inconvenient time.

As soon as Pauline opened the door, Woodrow rudely zipped past her without acknowledging her presence.

"Hey, Pop. What can I do for ya?" Samuel dryly asked.

"Son, I need a favor from you!"

Samuel looked at his father as if he'd told him he was dying from prostate cancer. He wasn't used to his father asking him for favors. He was immune to his father's constant harsh criticisms, but being asked a favor by his father was very foreign.

"I need you to visit Sista Rosetta at the nursing home tomorrow morning, because I plan to go fishing with two of the deacons from Holy Mary's Catholic

Church." Woodrow's favor sounded more like an
order.

"Pop, I have a sermon to do tomorrow and I plan to
take Pauline and Chastity out for dinner afterward.
Pauline and I haven't been spending enough quality
time together lately. Shouldn't your visit with Rosetta
take priority over fishing with the other pastors?"
Samuel shocked himself with his last sentence, because
he never questioned his father.

Even though Samuel was a grown man with his own
family, he was still somewhat intimidated by his father.
Woodrow was a no-nonsense disciplinarian and a
pastor. Samuel's mother had died when he was born
and Woodrow had to raise him on his own. Woodrow
made sure that his son was in church every single day.
Whenever Samuel misbehaved, his father would beat
him with switches, punch him, and force him to read
and recite extensive passages from the Bible. Samuel
wasn't allowed to have friends growing up, and his
father made him to listen to Gospel music. Samuel
loved his father, but he hated him for every
punishment he'd subjected him to. He still had welt
scars on his back from the switches his father had
inflicted on him.

"Are you sassing me, boy?!"

14

"No, sir," Samuel replied and lowered his head as he clasped his hands behind his back.

"Young man, you are never too old to be disciplined. As long as I'm breathing, I'm still your father. Remember the scripture, 'Honor thy father and honor thy mother?' Well, you'd better act like you know! Tomorrow you're going down to that nursing home after church, and you're going to say a prayer for Sista Rosetta. Do I make myself clear, boy?" Woodrow's eyes were bulged out so far, they looked like they were going to fall out of their sockets.

He wasn't taking no for an answer. Samuel just stood there looking defeated. No one said anything for two seconds. That was when Pauline finally broke the ice.

"Daddy Woodrow, what Samuel's trying to say is that he works very hard and that he needs to spend time with me and our daughter. Honestly, it isn't fair for you to renege on your promise to Sista Rosetta by making Samuel pick up the slack."

"Umm, with all due respect, Pauline, my boy is the one I'm talking to—not you. So, I really see no reason for you to voice your opinion. I mean, he is the bread winner and the man."

"I beg your pardon?" Pauline snapped.

15

"I'm sure you heard me clearly, Pauline. Perhaps you need me to use sign language to get my point across," Woodrow retorted.

"Let me tell you one thing—" she started.

Samuel intervened and said, "Pauline, why don't you go into the kitchen and continue preparing supper?"

Before Pauline could protest, Samuel continued to speak and wouldn't allow her to get another word in edgewise. "Pauline, please! I'll handle it. Just go into the kitchen and continue preparing our meal, okay?"

When Samuel gave her a reassuring look, she shot a scowl at Woodrow, who was smirking like a Cheshire Cat. She cut her eyes at him and stomped off into the kitchen mumbling incoherently under her breath.

"Pop, you didn't have to be so mean to her."

"Look here, boy. You are the man of this house and she's the woman of this house. Her duty is to serve and obey you. Not question you or get into your manly business."

As Woodrow spoke, spit flew out of his mouth and specks of it landed on Samuel's upper lip. Samuel wiped it off with the cuff of his sleeve. He didn't reply immediately, because he was trying to choose his words wisely. He didn't want to say anything that would fuel his father's anger. "I love my wife. She is my rib and I treat her as an equal because she's an important aspect to our marriage. I love her and our daughter very much."

"Boy, let me tell you something. As soon as you give a woman too much power, she'll start bossing you around as if she's the one with a twig and berries between her thighs. It's bad enough these women think they can do anything a man can do." Samuel was about to speak up, but Woodrow silenced him before he could utter another word. "Boy, do not interrupt me while I'm talking."

"Sorry, sir," Samuel muttered and dropped his head like he used to do whenever her father would scold him for being disobedient.

"Now, as I was saying, ever since these women were granted the constitutional right to vote and be treated fairly, they've wanted to take over the world! If I had my way, they'd be at home, bare foot, pregnant, tending to their men, and in church every day. That's how it was during the biblical times, son. You of all people should know that. A woman should always know her place. Don't ever let your woman forget that. I didn't raise no wimp. I raised a man. Understood?"

Samuel didn't appreciate how his father pigeonholed women as servants. Listening to his father's chauvinistic views about women being inferiors was enough to make him want to strangle him. It wasn't like Samuel wasn't physically capable of doing it. He was five inches taller than his father and he outweighed him by a hundred pounds. Samuel was built like a gladiator on the outside, but he felt like the same timid little boy on the inside.

"Boy, look at me when I'm talking to you!"

Samuel obliged and gave his father full eye contact, like a soldier in training. It was times like these when Samuel despised his father for his callous and controlling behavior. Getting his manhood crushed by his father felt like a spit in the face. Woodrow's blunt words cut straight through the bone marrow.

The best thing Samuel could say was, "Yes, sir."

Woodrow changed the subject as if nothing had ever happened. "Where's my precious grand baby?"

"She's upstairs watching TV."

Woodrow shouted for Chastity as if he lived there. "Chastity, come down stairs, young lady. Your paw-paw is here!"

Chastity was downstairs within twenty seconds. "Paw-Paw!" she exclaimed. She ran to him and wrapped her skinny arms around his wide pot belly. You would have thought she'd spotted Santa Claus. Well, Woodrow was like Santa Claus to her, because whenever he saw her, he would always give her money or candy.

"How's my only grandbaby doing?" Woodrow asked and smiled so wide, you could see every last one of his teeth.

"I'm doing fine, Paw-Paw." Chastity was adorable with her two, thick, long ponytails. She was a ray of sunshine and she was the spitting image of her mother.

"Are you reading your Bible every day, young lady?"

"Yes, Paw-Paw," she innocently said.

"Good girl! Your paw-paw got something for you." Woodrow reached into his pocket and pulled out his wallet. His fished ten dollars out of it and handed it to her.

"Thank you, Paw-Paw!"

19

"You're welcome, doll." Woodrow gave Chastity a bear hug and kissed her on the forehead. "You be good!"

"Okay, Paw-Paw." Chastity was as happy as a lark and she skipped up the stairs.

It broke Samuel's heart to watch his father exhibit so much affection to his granddaughter, because Woodrow had never been that affectionate to Samuel when he was Chastity's age. All he ever did was beat him and belittle him. He never even called him by his first name. He always referred to him as "boy" or "son". He called him boy when he was mad at him and he called him son when he was happy about something, or wanted Samuel to do something for him. From a young age, Samuel promised himself he would never mistreat his future children the way his father mistreated him.

"When is your wife dropping that little rascal she's carrying?" Woodrow dryly inquired.

"She's two months pregnant. The baby is due to arrive on April 15th."

Woodrow released a grunt. Samuel wasn't sure what his father meant by that. "Well, she'd better have a boy this time because males are already outnumbered by females in this country. I mean, don't get me wrong; I love my granddaughter, but I'll be completely happy when I have a grandson. On my father's side, there were nothing but males. We Baker men usually only produce males. You and Pauline are going to have a boy!" Woodrow just wouldn't let up. He was talking as if he had the authority to decide which gender the baby was going to be. He was way out of line, and Samuel hoped he would leave as soon as possible. Fortunately, his prayers were answered. "Welp, like I said before, you'll be visiting Sista Rosetta while I'm fishing with the fellas. I'll make sure that you did what I told you to do. I'm going home to read my Bible. I won't be having dinner with you tonight. That wife of yours is pretty, but her cooking ain't worth feeding to the roaches." Woodrow chuckled at his own obnoxious comment.

Samuel wasn't amused. Good riddance, he thought.

"See ya later, son."

"See ya, Pop." Samuel was crushed.

He always allowed his father to get the best of him. In spite of him being one of the richest, most prominent and influential televangelists of his time, his father still had a way of making him feel like a squished centipede. Yep! Woodrow was a bona fide mood killer because Samuel had lost his appetite for dinner and sex. Those painful childhood memories sent chills down his spine. All he wanted to do was forget about his father's impromptu visit and go straight to bed.

Chapter 3

Lies...All Lies...

Samuel was standing behind the pulpit. His wife and daughter were sitting behind him cheering him on as he pulled out his handkerchief to wipe the perspiration off his forehead.

"One of our loyal members is a God-fearing woman. She's been a member of our church for twenty years and she has a testimony she would like to share with the rest of the church. Sista Albertina, please stand up."

When Albertina stood up, the rest of the members clapped their hands in unison. Albertina was a sixty something year old woman who was built like a sumo wrestler. The wig on her head was lopsided and her window-like glasses practically covered her pudgy face. She stood up with her cane in her hand and revealed a toothless smile.

Samuel stepped down from his pulpit and approached her. He kissed her cheek and handed her a microphone.

"How are you feeling today, Sista Albertina?"

Albertina held the microphone to her dry and cracked lips. Her hand was shaking a little. "I feel alright, I guess. A few days ago, the doctor diagnosed me with breast cancer. He told me the cancer had spread all over my body and that there ain't nothin' else he can do." The tears poured down Albertina's face. Her lips trembled and she drooled a little.

"Sista Albertina, today is your lucky day. When you walk out of that door, you'll be cured of cancer. God is working his miracle on you as we speak," Samuel said. He glared into the camera and continued, "For everyone who's watching, I want you to pray for this beloved Sista." Samuel placed his hand on Albertina's forehead and said a prayer.

The church members bowed their heads and said silent prayers also.

"Father, one of your children is dying from cancer. She needs your help, and no one can heal her except you. As you know, doctors make mistakes because they're humans too. Lord, you are the true healer and

24

you are the one who can remove this cancer. Almighty God, please remove this cancer and kick it to the curb. Cancer, I rebuke you. I rebuke yoouuuuuuuu in the name of Jesus!" Samuel said dramatically.

Albertina collapsed and was caught by one of the ushers. Since Albertina was a hefty woman, she needed more than one usher to help break her fall. Hundreds of the members were crying, speaking in tongue, and praying.

Samuel announced the names of a few more members he wanted to bless. "Brotha Baines, stand up and tell the Lord what's on your mind." Samuel passed the microphone to the young man.

The young man had tattoos on his face and the matted locs on his head looked like a wooly cactus. He stood up and said, "I was released from prison three months ago, and now I can't find anyone who wants to hire me. I'm tired of people slamming the door in my face. Sometimes I think about killing myself."

"Say no more, young brotha. The Lord just told me that you'll receive a phone call regarding a job offer tomorrow morning." Samuel touched the young man's forehead and he collapsed. "Sista Beatrice, stand up and testify to the Lord."

Beatrice was a svelte, attractive brunette. She spoke in a nasally Barbie-like voice. "I'm bulimic and I make myself throw up. I'm tired of feeling fat and unattractive. I just want to be happy and healthy again." She erupted into tears.

Just as he'd done the other members who testified, Samuel touched her forehead, causing her to fall into one of the usher's arms. By then, people were milling around the church fainting and crying. The whole scene looked like a massacre, and it was being watched by millions of viewers around the world. Samuel was appalled by the sight. He battled the urge to walk out of the church and never look back. He looked behind him and saw his wife and daughter praying and crying like they were at a funeral.

It was unfair that his father had gone fishing while Samuel was left to preach to thousands of people. Deep down inside, Samuel didn't want to be there. He wanted to spend valuable time with his family, but his father threw a monkey wrench into his plans. If Samuel had had the power to make himself disappear in one poof, he would have done it at the snap of a finger. He looked around at the congregation once more and shook his head.

All of these people are idiots! Don't they know that the people whose names I called are nothing but paid actors? Is this the best Jesus Christ has to offer? Empty promises and deceit? he wondered to himself.

Samuel really wanted to tell all of them to go home because he was slowly growing tired of shamming them. For some odd reason, he hadn't been feeling like a Christian or a patriot lately. Rest assured, he was about to find out why he was harboring those feelings, and it was something prayer couldn't fix…

Chapter 4

Jesus, What Have I Done?

The drive home felt like an eternal one. Samuel was pensive and quiet as he drove Pauline and Chastity home. At first, all three of them were going to go see Rosetta, but Chastity kept complaining about how hungry she was. Samuel was rushing to get them home because he had to visit Rosetta within the next hour.

"You and I need to have a talk about Daddy Woodrow," Pauline blurted.

"About what? Why?" Samuel was in no mood for confrontation.

"Samuel, you already know why," Pauline frustratingly said.

Samuel wasn't in a talking mood. He had enough on his mind about Christianity and being a so-called man of the cloth. The last thing he wanted to discuss was his cruel father.

"Sure, but can we discuss this when I come back from visiting Sista Rosetta?"

"That's fine with me. But you're not going to slide out of this one like you did with that Pastor Kerney Thomas minstrel show." She folded her arms and pursed her lips.

Chastity was too preoccupied with her new Nintendo DS game to notice the tension between her parents...

~~ ~~

As soon as the three of them entered the house, Samuel's cell phone chimed. He quickly removed the phone from his holster. The caller ID displayed the church's phone number.

"Hello?"

"Pastor Baker, it's Nina."

Nina was the senior secretary at the church. She didn't sound very happy. She wasn't her usual chipper self. Samuel knew something was wrong. "Hi, Nina; is everything okay? You don't sound very well."

"You're absolutely right, Pastor Baker. I'm sorry to be the carrier of bad news, but—" Nina paused and sniffled, "Sista Rosetta passed away ten minutes ago.

Her granddaughter called and told me that one of the nurses found her at the table with her face in a bowl of tomato soup. She stopped breathing. She was such a sweet old woman." Nina sniffled again.

Samuel almost laughed at the part about Rosetta's face falling into her soup when she took her last breath. He couldn't get that image out of his head.

"Rosetta lived a long and productive life. God has called her to glory. She's already watching us from above. It's going to be hard for me, but I'll announce it to the congregation on Tuesday."

Samuel was playing along. Since he was the face and pastor of the church, he had to act as if he really cared. What he was really thinking was, Rosetta was a ninety-year-old hag. She lived a long and productive life. It's not like her life was cut short. Of course, he wouldn't let Nina hear his true feelings.

Rosetta had been a member of the World Faith Missionary Baptist Church since it had opened. Before that, she'd been a member of his father's church from the day it opened as well. She was well respected, and she had been like the grandmother of the church. He couldn't wait until the news about her death blew over, because he wanted to get the whole boring thing over with.

"You're absolutely right, Pastor. Sista Rosetta is now at peace. She'll forever be missed, but she's in a better place." Nina was no longer crying and she sounded like her original self again.

"I'll work on a eulogy for her, but in the meantime, why don't you relax and take your mind off her demise. You should think about the wonderful contributions she made to the church and the community. Not only did she see history, but she was a part of it. I'm sure she would want everyone to be happy rather than mope about her passing away." Samuel loathed every word he said. He could care less about Rosetta. As far as he was concerned, Rosetta was just one less old geezer on the planet.

Pauline overheard his discourse with Nina. She stood by him and shook her head.

"I feel a whole lot better now, Pastor Baker. Sista Rosetta was loved by so many people, but once you deliver that powerful eulogy, you're going to have them shouting and giving glory to God. Have a good evening and I'll see you Tuesday." Nina hung up.

Samuel was glad to hear Nina was happy again, but he was more happy that he no longer had to visit Rosetta or discuss anything that pertained to her. Unfortunately, he did have to write a eulogy.

Screw it! I'll improvise a eulogy for her old dead ass, he thought.

In fact, that was the same attitude he'd been having toward his sermons lately. Rather than write stale sermons, he improvised them instead.

"Oh wow, Sista Rosetta's gone?" Pauline asked.

Samuel had become so lost in his thoughts, he'd forgotten that Pauline was standing nearby. "Yeah, umm, she passed away this morning." He feigned a sad face. "God rest her beautiful soul. She's now in good hands and she will be missed."

Pauline stared blankly and smiled. Her eyes glazed over, and that's when the tears begin to flow down her face.

Samuel stood there and envisioned Rosetta's face being in a bowl of tomato soup. He chuckled to himself. He had no intentions of ever telling Pauline how Rosetta had really died. He was afraid he'd explode into laughter if he told her. He was so ready to change the subject.

"Well, I wanted to continue our discussion, but since Sista Rosetta's gone, you probably need some time to collect your thoughts," Pauline said.

"I'm fine, and I'm sure Sista Rosetta wouldn't mind either. By the way, where's Chastity?" he replied.

"She's in the kitchen eating a sandwich."

"I'm going to work on a eulogy for Sista Rosetta," he lied.

"Sure, that's fine. We can talk later. I'll go check on Chastity."

"Okay," he said. Samuel waited until Pauline disappeared into the kitchen, then he quickly ran to his office and shut the door. He really wanted to lock it, but he knew if Pauline decided to stop by his office while the door was locked, she'd get suspicious and catch the wrong idea; so he left it unlocked instead.

He was dying to do some sleuthing on the truth about Christianity via YouTube and Google. He'd been asking himself a lot of questions regarding Christianity and the Illuminati, because he'd been hearing so much about the Illuminati and the mark of the beast. He didn't know much about either one, but he was determined to find out. He turned on his computer, and as soon as he started to log on, Woodrow barged into his office and startled the death out of him. Luckily, the door wasn't locked.

"What's the matter, boy? You look like you saw the grim reaper," his father remarked.

The audacity of Woodrow to waltz into his son's house without calling him first was outrageous. Just days ago, his father had stopped by unannounced, and ruined an intimate evening for him and Pauline. To top it off, he'd demanded that Samuel visit Rosetta at the nursing home, then downgraded Samuel's manhood and insulted Pauline's cooking. Now, he'd taken it upon himself to enter Samuel's office without knocking.

Samuel fought the urge to scream and go nuts on his father for being so inconsiderate and churlish. Instead, he kept his composure. "What can I do for you, Pop?"

"Your wife let me in and told me you were in your office. Boy, you must have given her a good tongue lashing last night. 'Cause as soon as she saw me, she told me you were in your office and continued her womanly duties. It's about time you grew some balls and showed her who's boss. I'm proud of ya boy." Woodrow sniggered and sat back in the chair soaking up the ambience in the office.

How could she let this muthafucka come into my office without speaking to me first? She is equally the woman of this house as I'm the man of this house. As soon as this Bible-thumping bastard leaves my house, she and I are going to have a much needed discussion. Samuel shook his head. "What can I do for you, Pop?" he asked again. He wanted to be as diplomatic as possible.

"I heard about Sista Rosetta. I'm gon' miss that woman. She was a saint. I'm gon' miss her homemade peach cobbler too." Woodrow looked starry-eyed as he reminisced about the old woman.

"I was about to write a eulogy for her when you came in." Samuel despised lying to his father and wife, but it was the only thing that veiled his true feelings and thoughts.

"You just be sure to write a decent eulogy. Sista Rosetta was a fine woman and she don't deserve no sloppy eulogy. So don't be half-stepping when you eulogize her good name." Woodrow gave Samuel a stern look. It was like he could see through Samuel's soul with his creepy, bloodshot, beady eyes.

Samuel was growing agitated by the second. The nerve of this old grump to insult his work when he was the one who'd put 'fishing with the fellas' over visiting Rosetta on the day she kicked the bucket. "I'll give her a glowing eulogy. You can count on it," he said with forced enthusiasm.

"Good." Woodrow released a loud burp and didn't excuse himself. His burp smelled like he'd consumed spoiled hog head cheese with onions.

Samuel grimaced at his father's lack of manners. For someone who was a self-professed man of God, Woodrow had just as much civility as a dung beetle.

"Well, son, I don't want to hold you up any longer. I'm gonna let you get back to writing that eulogy. Oh, and when you finish it, I want to see it before you read it to the congregation. I want to make sure it's perfect."

For crying out loud! Samuel almost blurted what he was thinking. "Sure, Pop," he said instead and sighed.

Woodrow got up and left without even saying goodbye. Samuel sat in silence and shook his head for a moment. Then he suddenly slammed his fist on his desk. He was furious. Woodrow was like a skinworm that had gotten under his skin. He wasn't startled like he'd been with Woodrow when Pauline suddenly entered the room.

Samuel gave her a disapproving look. "How come you didn't speak to me before allowing him to grace my office with his unwanted presence?" Samuel snarled.

"Well, since I'm only the mother and the wife of this house, my views don't count. My role in this relationship is to cook, clean, raise our daughter and speak when I'm spoken to." Pauline's comments were dripping with sarcasm.

"Come on, Pauline. You know that isn't true. You and Chastity mean a lot to me."

Pauline released a derisive laugh. "Oh, really? Apparently, you agree with your father, because you never apologized or mentioned his rudeness the other night. I overheard the entire conversation. All you did was go to bed, wake up, and act like it never happened."

"Obviously, you weren't listening closely, because I told him how much I love you and Chastity. I told him you're my rib and how much you mean to me."

"Yes, but you stood there and allowed him to trash me after you defended me. You even let him stomp all over your manhood."

Samuel was getting tired of Pauline's nagging. If she'd been created with a built-in pause button, he would have pressed it and left her standing there looking like a mannequin.

"Sweetheart, you know how he is. We've been married for eight years now. You should be accustomed to his behavior. I don't know why you're acting brand new about this."

Pauline gave him a glower that he'd never seen before. Her yellow-brown eyes turned black. "How dare you condone that old brute's behavior? I've watched and listened to that man verbally attack you and our marriage for years. Every night I pray that he comes to terms with our marriage and our daughter. I know he gives me dirty looks when I'm not looking. I'm not stupid, you know. It's amazing how he misuses the Scriptures when he's everything the Bible speaks against!"

Samuel remained silent. He wanted to see where Pauline was going with her tirade. "You want to know what's sad? I'll tell you. It's sad that I've never seen you stand up to your father. Last night, when you asked him why he wouldn't visit Sista Rosetta, I thought you were finally going to give him a piece of your mind. When you failed to do it, you really disappointed me. I should have known that you'd never stand up to him, because you're a coward!" Pauline spat and pointed at Samuel. Pauline had never spoken to him that way before. Despite every little argument they'd had, she'd never berated him. Samuel was sort of surprised by her behavior, and worse, her calling him a coward.

He carefully said, "I am not a coward. I'm a pacifist, alright?"

Pauline cackled again. "Pacifist?" she said mockingly as if she'd never heard of the word. "Even pacifists stand their ground! Your father is right; you are a wimp!" she continued.

"You know what, Pauline? You'd better leave before I end up saying something I'll regret."

Pauline didn't budge. She continued treading on his patience. "Gosh, Samuel; if you had the balls to stand up to your father the way you're standing up to me now, your father would have more respect for you and our marriage." Pauline laughed like she was the bride of Satan.

Samuel's blood started boiling. His temperature was so hot, it could've burst a thermometer. He rose from his seat and pointed his finger at her. "Pauline, that's enough. Cut it out now!"

Pauline ignored him and continued taunting him. "Aww, what's the matter, Sammy, baby? Can't handle the truth? You're built like the Hulk, and you have it big between the legs, but you have no balls!"

Before Pauline could utter another insult, Samuel yanked her by the collar of her maternity blouse. "Shut the fuck up, bitch! If you ever disrespect me like that again, I'll rip your goddamn tongue out of your mouth and bitch slap you with it!" he roared.

Pauline was gasping for air. He quickly released his grip on her collar and she began crying as she tried to regain her breath.

"Pauline, I'm so sorry," Samuel said as he finally came back to reality.

Pauline stormed out of the room, went into the bathroom across the hallway and slammed the door.

"I'm sorry, baby! I didn't mean to grab you and cuss you! Please come out so we can talk," Samuel begged as he followed her to the bathroom and turned the doorknob; it was locked. He knocked but Pauline didn't respond. He heard her sobbing and sniffling through the door.

"Baby, I'm sorry. I don't know what came over me. You know I would never hit you."

There was still no answer from Pauline.

"Baby, please talk to me. Lord as my witness, I'll never threaten to hit you again." The sobs grew louder. Samuel acquiesced and returned to the bedroom. He was mad at himself. He was so mad, he punched himself in the chest twice before he sat in his chair. "Jesus, what have I done?"

In the eight years they'd been married, none of their arguments had ever escalated to this degree. Samuel had never been violent with his wife. He was stunned by his reaction and he wished he could rewind the incident and handle it differently. He loved his wife and would never touch a single strand of hair on her body. He knew he was wrong for what he'd done, but he blamed his father for the whole thing. Pauline was right for calling him a wimp, because had he stood up to his father a long time ago, their argument would have never occurred.

What was worse was that Samuel condemned domestic violence in his sermons, yet he was doing what he preached against. Being a pastor was taking its toll on him. Samuel knew he needed to do something before someone ended up getting hurt. He'd behaved worse than his myopic minded father. Samuel was growing tired of the whole Christian and holier-than-thou façade.

Chapter 5

Making Up

Samuel spent the night on the couch in his office. Due to him grabbing Pauline, he'd felt guilty about sleeping in the same bed with her. He hadn't showered, and his scruffy five o'clock shadow made an overnight appearance. He desperately wanted to hold her and apologize for losing his cool. To his surprise, he heard a knock at the door.

"Come in," he said.

"Are you sure I can come in?" a voice asked meekly from the other side of the door.

"Of course you can," he replied.

It was Pauline. She walked into the room and shut the door. The two of them exchanged glances. The tension in the room was so thick, it could choke a fly on the wall. Samuel stood up with outstretched arms, and Pauline ran into them and cried like a baby.

"Baby, I'm sorry for the terrible things I said to you. You're a good husband and you're a good father." Pauline buried her head in his chest.

"Sweetheart, it's not your fault. I was the one who grabbed you. I'm the one who owes you an apology."

Pauline stared at him with tear-filled eyes and shook her head. "I provoked you, Samuel. I was clearly out of line and I promise I'll never speak to you that way again," Pauline cried out and reburied her face in Samuel's chest.

"It's okay, Pauline." Samuel gently rubbed her back, chucked her under the chin, and looked straight into her beautiful eyes. "Darling, we all make mistakes and you were right about me not standing up to my father. I should work on that. My father is a firm man, but it doesn't exempt him from taking shots at you or me. I need to work on my relationship with my father. It's going to be tough, but that's the chance I'm willing to take for my family. Eventually, my dad will have to realize that I'm a grown man with my own life and family now. I promise I'll never grab you out of anger again. I love you, Mrs. Baker."

"I love you too, Mr. Baker."

The two kissed each other hungrily and they started undressing each other. They made passionate love on the floor like never before...

~~ ~~

When Samuel woke up, Pauline was still sleeping serenely; she looked so beautiful when she slept. Samuel didn't want to wake her up. He slowly got up and put his pants back on.

He approached his desk where his computer sat and logged on. Google was his default browser page and once it loaded, he typed, the truth about Christianity into the search field. He eased into his chair while he waited for the results to pop up. There were so many results to choose from. He clicked on a particular link and another window opened up. He scrolled down the page with the cursor and suddenly saw something that piqued his interest. It was about Constantine. He heard Pauline squirming around. He hurriedly bookmarked the page so he wouldn't lose it.

"Samuel," Pauline groggily said while sitting up.

Samuel immediately closed the browser. He didn't want to alarm her in any fashion. Pregnancy had a way of making a woman emotional and hormonal. He shot up from his desk to help her up off the floor.

"Hello, beautiful."

"Hello, handsome."

Samuel guided her from the floor. They gave each other a peck on the lips.

"What were you looking at on the internet?"

"I was viewing the church's website," he lied.

"Oh okay. Would you like for me to make you lunch?" Pauline asked as she wrapped her arms around Samuel's neck and kissed him on his dimpled square chin.

"Sure, baby; but I have to take a shower first."

"While you're taking a shower, I'll prepare lunch for you."

"Thanks, baby." Samuel gave her another peck on the lips.

~~   ~~

A short while later, Samuel stepped out of the shower; it had felt invigorating and liberating, and he felt renewed and relieved. He opened the medicine cabinet and pulled out his shaving cream. He closed the cabinet, and wiped the fog off the mirror. When he looked into the mirror, he dropped his can of shaving cream in the sink. He saw a reflection of himself with a foot-long scraggly beard, and his hair was in locs.

His reflection gave him a hard, cold stare and said, "Samuel, it's time for you to face the truth."

"Who are you? Are you me? Am I you?" Samuel was flummoxed out of his wits.

"I am your future, your conscience, and your voice," his reflection authoritatively said.

"I'm afraid I don't understand what you mean." Samuel was baffled.

"You are alive in the flesh, but you are spiritually dead. You are a wealthy preacher-pimp who rapes people for tithe money and you dumb down their senses with all that "Jesus" jazz. You know it's wrong, but it's your livelihood. It's something you've been conditioned to do since birth."

"I want to leave this life so badly, but it's like a drug habit that I can't seem to kick to the curb. I'm a best-selling author and a rich televangelist; how am I supposed to walk away from this life? It feels so wrong, but it's so rewarding at the same time. I can't just walk away from everything, because if I do, how am I going to support myself? This is all I know. What about my family and friends?" Samuel searched his future image's face for answers.

His reflection spoke with sound authority.

"Brotha, you are one lost soul. Money and fame are the least of your problems. The truth is everything you need. Your friends and money won't be able to spare you from the wrath of the true, almighty Yahawah. Your friends are not your real friends. As soon as the fortune and fame is gone, you'll become an afterthought to them. Do you think you're doing a good deed by upholding this wicked constitution and that pagan religion called Christianity? Ha! You have signed your death certificate, my friend." Samuel's image laughed at him so hard, his laughter echoed.

It was like Samuel was watching a horror movie starring his double, in the mirror. "Is it too late for me to pray for redemption? How do I seek the truth?"

"You must first read the original King James Version from Genesis to Revelation; it talks about the Hebrew Israelites—the real Israelites."

"Is that all?"

"That is all."

"What about my career and everything around me?"

"I told you everything you need to know. It is up to you to chase the truth. Shalom." Samuel's doppelgänger vanished into thin air.

"Wait, don't go!" Samuel sighed and saw his present self appear in the mirror again. "Original King James Version," he repeated to himself. He was shook up by what he'd witnessed. He quickly donned his robe. He didn't want to shave now because he was afraid he would cut himself due to what he'd seen.

He descended the stairs to the kitchen, ready to eat lunch. He entered the kitchen without saying anything. Pauline was preparing him a tuna bagel sandwich with apple slices.

"Hey honey, how was your shower?"

Samuel was lost in thought and didn't respond. He couldn't stop pondering what he'd seen.

"Samuel, are you okay?" Pauline gave Samuel a puzzled look.

"Oh, uh…yeah, I'm fine. I was thinking about Sista Rosetta. God, I'm going to miss that woman." Samuel feigned a phony smile.

"Aww, honey, I'm sorry. I totally know how you feel. She was a heavenly woman and I'm going to miss her too. She could probably walk on water. God was good to her."

Samuel wasn't in the mood to engage in any more sad talk about Rosetta. Rosetta was the last person on his mind and Samuel knew he wasn't going to miss her. She and his father were close, therefore, his father should be the one jumping through hoops to prepare her funeral service instead.

"Yes, she was a fine woman. I'm going to miss her," he repeated, while thinking, Noooottttt!

Samuel changed the subject. "This tuna sandwich is delicious. You really outdid yourself." He munched on his bagel sandwich and relished the savory flavor.

"Not as well as I outdid myself this morning," Pauline teased.

"Woman, you'd better stop before we have a round four in this kitchen." They both laughed.

"Uh-uh, that's how we ended up making this one that's growing inside of me," Pauline laughed.

"I'm sure we're going to have a boy this time," Samuel said as he rubbed Pauline's stomach.

"That's something your dad would say." She sucked her teeth playfully and rolled her eyes.

Samuel laughed again. "Yes, that is true, but wouldn't it be nice if we had a junior running around here?"

"Whatever sex the baby is, is fine by me. All I want is a healthy baby." She smiled and rubbed her stomach.

"Yeah, but can I at least pray for a boy?" Samuel joshed while rubbing her belly.

"Samuel, you are something else. I guess that's why I love you so much," Pauline laughed.

"When is your next checkup?"

"The next checkup is next Friday afternoon at two o'clock. Etta-Rose is going to attend it with me."

Etta-Rose was Samuel and Pauline's housekeeper and nanny. She was currently on a seven day vacation with her family in Wild Hog, Kentucky. She was originally from New Orleans, but after Hurricane Katrina claimed her job, home, and most of her family members, she relocated to Miami to start her life all over again. Samuel hired her through a temp agency and the rest was history. Etta-Rose had been working for them for four years now, and she was like family;

she treated Chastity like the granddaughter she'd never had.

"Have you heard from Etta-Rose lately?" Samuel inquired.

"She left a message on my voicemail this morning. She said she's having a good time with her folks. But she said she misses us a lot, especially Chastity."

"I miss her too. That woman makes the best red velvet muffins in Miami," Samuel said while mentally relishing the flavor of the red velvet muffins.

"She sure does. But it's great that she's spending time with her family, because she's honest, God-fearing, and she works very hard," Pauline exclaimed.

"She most certainly does. In fact, I've been thinking about giving her another raise. Don't you agree?" Samuel added.

"I totally agree and I'm sure she would agree too," Pauline replied and beamed.

"Great! When she returns from her vacation, I'll let her know," Samuel said as he took another large bite out of his tuna sandwich.

"Sounds good to me," Pauline replied. "How is the eulogy coming along?"

"It's coming along very well," Samuel lied again. He hadn't given that eulogy a second thought, let alone Rosetta's death.

"I can't wait to hear it during service."

Samuel ignored Pauline's last comment. He was getting tired of hearing the name Rosetta and anything that sounded like it. He wanted to squash the whole thing and move on; furthermore, he was growing tired of the whole church scene. All he wanted to do was rest and forget about work.

"So, how about we continue our session before we pick up Chastity?" Samuel snaked his arms around Pauline's expanding waistline and gave her a knowing look.

"I thought you'd never mention it." Pauline said and giggled devilishly.

Samuel picked her up, carried her out of the kitchen and up the stairs.

The Bold and the Ugly Truth

Chapter 6

*Here We Go Again *Sigh**

Samuel was in his office at the church. He had 45 minutes remaining before he went on air. He logged on to his computer to look up the website about Constantine that he'd bookmarked earlier. Before he could pull the site up, he heard a knock at the door.

Who the fuck is it now?! He wanted to tell whoever the person was at the door to go away.

"Come in!" he said.

It was Nina. "Pastor, I have Rosetta's granddaughter on the phone and she doesn't sound very happy. I told her you're getting ready for service, but she demanded to speak to you anyway. What should I tell her?" Nina asked while nervously biting her fingernails and looking wild-eyed.

Samuel sighed. "I have to prepare my sermon and my makeup artist is going to be here in ten minutes. Tell her I'll have to call her back after service."

"Okay," Nina said and frantically closed the door.

Samuel wondered what had Rosetta's granddaughter so uptight. Whatever was on her mind would have to wait until service ended. He usually wouldn't see anyone unless they scheduled an appointment with Nina first. Samuel was a thorough man who did everything by the book—his book. No parishioner was treated better than the other. Everyone had to adhere to his policy, and that applied to Rosetta's granddaughter as well.

Samuel logged off his computer and immersed himself in his thoughts. The reflection of his future self that he'd seen in the mirror resurfaced to the front of his mind again. Was he ready to introduce his true self to the world so soon? It was true he was growing weary of being a man of the cloth and everything that pertained to church. Yes, he'd amassed wealth, power, and fame, but something about the whole thing perturbed him. Becoming a pastor, was not what he'd had in mind—it had been his father's idea. Samuel wanted to be a paramedic. When he'd told his father he wanted to help save lives while riding in the back of a wagon, his father had come down on him like the Apocalypse. Woodrow wasn't having it any other way. He'd twisted Samuel's ear, made him put his hand on the

Bible, and told him to promise to never utter blasphemy against the Lord again.

It was a harrowing experience for young Samuel. Woodrow was a tough parent; he would put on a front for his followers, friends, and neighbors. But when he was at home, he was the big bad wolf. He was scary enough to make Joe Jackson look like the Pope. There were times when Samuel had prayed for his own demise, because he'd been brainwashed to believe he was a failure in the eyes of God, and that he would never amount to anything higher than his head. Twenty years later, he had a loving family of his own and an enviable lifestyle. But he was miserable like an old woman who lived alone with her twenty cats. Thanks to his tetchy father, Samuel was thriving off the hard-earned dollars of his minions. While they were foraging and scraping for every penny they earned, he was basking in the opulence of his wealth, courtesy of their hard work and ignorance. He'd been mentored by a few of his predecessors, along with some of the professors at his biblical college. They'd all trained and molded him into a figure of deception and thievery. The bile climbed up his esophagus and it left a slimy sour taste on his tongue. It was downright sickening, and he didn't know how much longer he could stomach the shenanigans.

There was a knock at his door. "Come in."

It was his make-up artist. "Hello, Pastor. How are you today?"

"Things couldn't be better, Tasha. How are you today?"

"I'm blessed, praise the Lord."

Samuel rolled his eyes at Tasha's last comment, but she didn't catch it.

Tasha was a 21-year-old art student and a reputable celebrity make-up artist. She worked with a bevy of celebrities such as, Taraji Henson, Kandi Burress, Nia Long, Thandie Newton, and the list continued. Tasha opened her personal make-up kit and went to work on Samuel's face.

Samuel admired Tasha's work ethics. She was punctual and she delved in on what he paid her to do—less small talk, no play. It was that crucial. Another thing that was disturbing his conscience was wearing make-up. He secretly cringed at the thought of it because it made him feel feminine. And not only that, but Tasha had a smattering of male clients, although the majority of her clientele were females. Image was one thing, but wearing makeup was beginning to chip away at his manhood. And his judgmental father wasn't doing his manhood any justice, either.

I don't know why I have to wear this sissy ass make-up. I'm a naturally fine ass man, he thought.

Samuel was indeed eye candy. He was attractive enough to make a blind woman see. All the women at his church checked him out. Samuel had been among the top five on People Magazine's "Sexiest Men Alive" roster. He'd ranked number two, behind Johnny Depp. George Clooney was number three, Blair Underwood was number four, and Denzel Washington was number five.

Samuel was facially and financially blessed to have any woman he desired. The only reason he'd never committed adultery was because of his father. As a child, Samuel had watched his father bring different women into his house, lust them down, give them money, and send them on their way. Samuel often repented for his sins, but most of all, he prayed to never become anything like his hypocritical father.

"All done," Tasha sang and handed him a mirror.

"Thanks, Tasha; you're amazing." Samuel examined his face in the mirror.

"I know." Tasha couldn't help but smile at her incredible work. She was beside herself.

"I look like a bitch-made, punk ass, pussy, fag boy," he wanted to say.

"See you at the pulpit, Pastor Baker," Tasha cheerfully said and started collecting and securing her cosmetic belongings.

"You most certainly will," he replied.

Samuel slid on his pulpit robe, plastered a phony smile on his face, and braced himself for another dreadful sermon...

~~   ~~

"How is everyone doing today?!" Samuel shouted at the congregation.

"We're blessed, Pastor Baker!" shouted a freckled face, fair-skinned, blue haired old lady in the front pew.

Samuel slowly paced around the space he was in. He clutched the microphone and looked back at Pauline and Chastity. Pauline mouthed, "I love you" and Chastity gave him a huge lollipop smile. He redirected his eyes to the massive congregation and cleared his throat. He wanted to cuss out the camera man and tell him where to deposit his camera.

Why the hell am I doing this? I don't give ten buckets of cow piss about that dead old wench. I wish I could say fuck it and walk away from this shit, for good!

Samuel took a deep breath and cleared his throat again. "One of our beloved church members passed away last week. Many of us knew her as Sista Rosetta. She passed away in the nursing home."

Murmurs of regret could be heard as most of the congregation cried. "Sista Rosetta isn't dead. She's now resting peacefully and eternally. That is why we must keep her legacy alive through ourselves, the church, and our children," Samuel continued.

"Amen!" the congregation shouted.

"Sista Rosetta was a woman of magnanimity, honor, and grace!" Samuel said with animation.

"Yes, she was!" shouted a twenty-something year old willowy, olive skin girl.

"Not only was Sista Rosetta a valued member of this church and my father's, she shared stomping grounds with Reverend Dr. Martin Luther King Jr, Coretta

Scott King, and Rosa Parks! And she helped pave the way for every last one of us!"

The pianist struck a tune on the organ.

"Amen, brotha. Preach on!" a wiry-haired moon-faced man shouted.

"Sista Rosetta should have a museum, street, and a charm school named after her because she was the epitome of elegance. No, y'all don't hear me!" Samuel enunciated.

The pianist started playing shouting music, and the rest of the band followed his lead. More shouting ensued and church members began running up and down the aisle. Many of them were break-dancing, pop-locking, doing the split, the worm, the robot, the Dougie, and the holy ghost dance. Pauline and Chastity were clapping and singing.

Samuel witnessed one of the parishioners passed out on the floor and shuddered; her private parts were exposed. Her scruffy vagina looked like a wooly mammoth's eyelids. Three of the other female members were fanning her and trying to cover her up. He hoped the camera crew didn't catch it.

This nasty ass broad isn't wearingany panties!
Goodness fucking gracious! I think I'm going to be
sick, he thought to himself.

Samuel had never seen anything so disturbing in all of
his years behind the pulpit. He was appalled and
flummoxed by the response to the eulogy and the
scene unfolding in front of him.

These coons are break dancing in the church like
they're in a dance-off contest. They might as well
swing on vines, drum on watermelons, and eat
bananas too! Samuel felt a migraine brewing. He
massaged his temples and squeezed his eyes tight.

"Okay, folks. I want all of you to settle down and go
back to your respective pew!" he yelled with force.
What he really wanted to say was, "Sit your silly, spear
chucking, monkey asses down."

The majority of the members gave him a bemused
look because it was unlike him to tell them to stop so
abruptly. They usually spent ten minutes prancing,
dancing, and jumping around the church like
incorrigible children on speedballs. Then, Samuel
would delve into one of the scriptures from the Bible,
and they would stop. But that day, Samuel was in no
mood for coonery, loonery, or bafoonery.

"I want all of you to take out your Bible." The headache was drumming so loud and hard, he was afraid the audience was going to hear it. Then he proceeded to deliver the worst sermon he'd ever preached...

After the worship service was over, Samuel ran into his office, ripped off his robe, popped two aspirin into his mouth, and sucked down the bottle of water on his desk. He was in no mood to speak or shake hands with any of the parishioners. He was sweating profusely and he loosened the tie around his neck.

"What a damn day. If I don't get away from here, I'm going to explode!" he muttered to himself.

Nina entered the room. Samuel had forgotten to close the door. "That was a powerful sermon you gave, Pastor."

"Thanks, Nina," Samuel dryly said.

"Is something wrong, Pastor Baker?" Nina asked with a fading smile.

"No, um, I just have a slight headache, that's all."

"Would you like for me to bring you some hot tea?"

"No thanks, Nina. I took two aspirin and they're working wonders," Samuel said with a pseudo smile.

"Well, if you need anything, I'm a holler away," she said and smiled again.

"Thanks, Nina."

Nina waved and closed the door on her way out. As soon as she was gone, so was Samuel's bogus smile. Samuel sat and powered up his laptop. Hopefully his father or wife wouldn't stop by to ask him a hundred thousand questions. Two minutes later, the door flew open.

"I need to talk to you!" the young woman standing in the doorway demanded.

That was when Nina rushed in behind the woman. "Pastor Baker, I tried to stop her, but she ignored me. I'm really sorry," Nina said in a defeated tone, as she clutched her cross and looked overwhelmed.

Samuel had forgotten to call Sista Rosetta's granddaughter back. He was growing tired of people flying into his office without knocking, especially his father. Samuel wanted to rip the young woman a new orifice, but he didn't want to show his true colors in front of Nina. He mustered up the most crisp voice he could find.

"Nina, it is okay. Don't be so hard on yourself. It's all my fault because I forgot about my phone appointment with Ms.—"

" It's Mrs. Nadine Burns," the woman hastily corrected and rolled her eyes.

"Mrs. Burns, I really apologize. It's just that—"

"It's just that you too busy shuckin' and jivin' in front of them cameras that you ignore the most important people you have appointments with. Negro, please!" Nadine dismissively waved him off and popped her gum with emphasis.

"Pastor Baker, is there anything else you need?" Nina timorously asked.

"No, Nina. That'll be all, thanks."

"Well, damn. You just gonna send yo' little secretary off without askin' me if I want anything? You rude as hell!" Nadine scolded, jerking back and giving Samuel a side-eyed look.

Samuel wanted to smack the gum and the taste out of her mouth. "I'm sorry, Ms. Burns. Would you like anything?"

"My name ain't Ms. Burns; it's Mrs. Burns, dammit. I'm a married ass woman!" Nadine shoved her hand in Samuel's face, displaying her wedding band. "And, no honey. I don't want nothin'. You dismissed," Nadine added as she dismissively waved without looking back at Nina.

Samuel nodded at Nina.

"Okay, Pastor." Nina quickly closed the door as if her life depended on it.

"What can I do for you, Mrs. Burns?"

Nadine ignored his question and fished out a cigarette and a book of matches. Samuel frowned at her and gave her a repulsive look. Not only was she spiritually ugly, but she was facially ugly too. Her face was flat, her chin hung lower than a pelican's, and her thin lips were dry and smut black.She was paper thin and her paper bag colored skin looked like she'd bathed in asphalt. Her raggedy hair extensions were clinging onto the tips of her nappy new growth and her black skirt looked like it had semen stains on it. She smelled like a mixture of cheap perfume, cigarettes, and dirty laundry, which explicated the white stains on her cheap skirt.

She lit up her cigarette and blew smoke rings in Samuel's face. Samuel swatted at the smoke, choking on it, but Nadine wasn't fazed. "I want my grandmama to have a big, fancy ass funeral. I don't want her layin' up in no coffin wearing no cheap ass wig or clothes either. She was a classy lady and I want her buried in style, ya feel me?" Nadine took a long pull on her cigarette.

Samuel coughed violently and handed her an ashtray. Nadine was still unfazed, ignored the ashtray, and continued. "My grandmama was a fine woman. Hell, she even left me a check for $75, 000. That's enough to cover the funeral expenses, but I'm gonna use that money for me and my boyfriend instead." Nadine was chewing her gum like cud and popping it loudly.

"Mrs. Burns, didn't you just say you're a married woman?" Samuel questioned with furrowed eyebrows.

"Yes, I did, and?" Nadine hissed and rolled her neck.

"And now you say you have a boyfriend?" Samuel said incredulously.

"So? What the hell that got to do with my grandmama's funeral?" Nadine huffily remarked. She pulled harder on her cigarette, and blew more smoke into his face.

Samuel bit his bottom lip. His patience was bursting at the seams and he hated cigarettes. "Will you kindly put the cigarette out, Mrs. Burns?" Samuel asked as he slid the ashtray closer to her.

Nadine sucked her teeth and obligingly put the cigarette out. "Is ya happy now?" she spat.

"Thank you," Samuel replied with a matching attitude and tone.

"Don't flatter yaself, negro. I ain't one for puttin' out no good ass cigarettes just to please fake ass holier-than-thou folks like you, who can't stand the smell of cigarettes. This is a free goddamn country."

Samuel ignored Nadine's scathing remarks once again and resumed where he'd left off. "Mrs. Burns, I only asked you an observatory question about your marital status. I wasn't judging you."

Nadine gave Samuel a perilous look. If looks could kill, Samuel would have been dead on arrival. "What I do ain't none of yo' goddamn business, and don't be flaunting them two hundred dollar words at me like I'm stupid or something. Since you tryna dig in my business, yeah I'm an adulteress. I have a sideline man, because my husband is servin' two years in prison for violating his parole. My sideline man treats me good and he pays all my bills. We both gonna spend all that money my grandmama left me, in the Bahamas. Satisfied?!" Nadine hissed while waving her index finger around in a ghetto girl like gesture and rolling her neck.

Samuel sighed and leaned his head onto the back of his chair. "Mrs. Burns, why are you here? What do you want from me?" he asked. He straightened his posture, looked her straight in the face and clasped his hands to avoid smacking her.

Nadine scowled. "Negro, do you need a damn hearing aid? I said I want a fancy ass funeral for my grandmama!"

"You told me what you wanted, but you didn't mention anything about paying for your grandmother's funeral," Samuel irritatingly said.

"Bingo! You just answered your own damn question," she yelled.

"Wait a second. Are you trying to say that you want this church to pay for Sista Rosetta's funeral?"

"Which part of, 'you answered your own damn question' don't you understand?" Nadine snapped as she chewed harder on her gum.

Samuel sighed and bit his lip again. "Ms. Burns—" he began.

"How many frickin' times I gotta say—"

"Whatever!" Samuel shot back, causing Nadine to jump a little. "I don't know what kind of games you're playing, but you will not barge into my office giving me demands in my own church. Your grandmother supposedly left you $75,000 to pay for her funeral. That money is not for you to go whoring on a Caribbean trip with a man who is not your husband. I refuse to address you by Mrs. Burns, because you do not act like a married woman or ladylike. You also owe my secretary an apology."

"Do you know who the hell you're talking to?" Nadine asked as she maneuvered to get into Samuel's face.

"Yes, I do. I'm talking to a selfish, demented, Jezebel whose deceased grandmother guilelessly left her in charge of her funeral and her money!" Samuel replied with disgust.

"Kiss my natural black ass!" Nadine lifted up her skirt, revealed her sagging buttocks and proceeded to shake them in his face. "Get a real good look, Pastor Pimp!" she snarled.

Samuel held up his hands to shield his eyes from her horror picture show of a booty. "Mrs. Burns, please! That is totally uncalled for; your behavior is utterly unacceptable and you are disrespecting the Lord. Pull your dress down this instant! What in the world is the matter with you, woman? I'm afraid I'm going to have to ask you to leave."

Nadine yanked her skirt down and faced Samuel. "Hell naw, you gon' hear me out first. You done disrespected me for the last time. Let me tell you somethin'; you don't know shit about me. It's easy for you church pimps to point y'all's fingers at folks, while you legally rip those same folks off at the same time. Y'all drive around in your fancy cars, own private planes, live in them big ass houses, wear designer clothes, and eat lobster and caviar while we po' folks struggle to survive. My grandmama was a member of yo' church and yo' pappy's church, which means she deserves more than a tired ass eulogy. I'ma spend that

$75,000 because I'm po' and I deserve it." Nadine was going off on one of her ghetto girl tangents. As she ranted, saliva flew out of her mouth.

Samuel had to admit that Nadine did have a point. He was fleecing the congregation and he and his family were living lavishly off the blood, sweat, and tears of his followers. But that fact didn't exempt Nadine from being a pimp either, because she was trying to hustle the church as well. And he wasn't going to concede to her accusations.

"You're only speaking about yourself, because you're the one who's trying to pimp the church. Your grandmother would be livid at you if she witnessed your disgusting behavior if she knew what you were doing. You're only doing the work of the devil."

"Negro, please! You the biggest con artist in television history. You have millions of viewers, millions of dollars, and a congregation of hos. You sell them miracle cloths that don't even work, and you find all sorts of ways to rape people by selling lies to 'em. The people you anoint are paid actors, so don't even feed me that bullshit, because my grandmama was one of yo' long-time loyal hos when she was livin'. But she will not be yo' ho' in death. This is why I never go to church, because it's jive turkey ass niggas like you who give Christianity a bad rep. I hope you all rot and burn in fuckin' hell!"

"You need to leave!" Samuel ordered.

"What's the matter, Pastor Pimp? Truth hurts, don't it? Tell ya what. I'm givin' you an ultimatum. If you don't pay for my grandmama's funeral, you gon' regret it."

"What the hell is that supposed to mean?" Samuel shot up from his chair faster than Freddy Krueger's switch blades.

Nadine was unnerved. She animatedly smirked, planted her hands on his desk, and leaned closer to him. "Let's just say, I know a crooked cop who likes to plant drugs on people, includin' crooked ass televangelists." Nadine winked and her smirk transformed into a wide smile, revealing her brown teeth, that had a front tooth missing.

"You, evil, maniacal bitch! That's blackmail," Samuel seethed and shook his fist.

"My, my, what a very foul mouth you have, Pastor Pimp! And FYI, it ain't blackmail, it's black female." Nadine sardonically laughed at her play on words.

"Get the hell out of my office, now!" Samuel boomed.

"With pleasure, Pastor Pimp." Nadine smacked on her gum, then blew it into a huge bubble until it popped. She continued smiling and she tried to straighten her wrinkled skirt with her hand as she pulled out another cigarette.

There was a knock at the door. "Come in!" Samuel bellowed."

I heard your exchange down the hallway. Is everything okay?" Nina asked in a worried voice.

"Everything is fine, Nina. Mrs. Burns was just leaving."

"Are you sure?" Nina looked at Samuel for reassurance and then at Nadine with frightened eyes.

"Yes, everything is fine. Would you please escort Mrs. Burns to the door, please?"

"I don't need no damn escort. I can do it myself." Nadine stepped toward the door and looked back at Samuel. "You just be sure to keep yo' end of the deal and we'll all be happy." Nadine popped her gum and winked at him once again. She sashayed to the door, sized up Nina, tooted her nose up, and continued her rhythmic strut down the hall.

Nina gave Samuel a puzzled look. "What was that all about, Pastor Baker?" Nina confusedly asked.

"It was nothing. Everything is fine. It's nothing for you to concern yourself about. Matter of fact, you can go home early today," Samuel replied.

"Oh…okay. Thanks, Pastor Baker," Nina said with a confused look and closed the door.

As soon as Nina closed the door, Samuel listened for her footsteps to disappear. Then he balled up his fist and punched a cantaloupe sized hole in the wall. "Goddamn, Jay Leno-looking, trifling, ghetto ass bitch!" He ran his trembling fingers through his hair and made a call to his longtime friend Roy.

Roy was a shady character he'd met while in college. Roy was never into anything legal. He either stole cars, or hacked into people's personal accounts and stole their identity. He'd been in and out of jail in the past, and once he'd been released from jail, he'd graduated to severe crimes. He took on a new life of selling drugs and he didn't mind taking another person's life if he needed to. He and Samuel were like night and day, and although Samuel wasn't a criminal, he was still guilty by association.

"Hey, Roy. Listen, man. I have a problem and I need you to help me get rid of it."

Chapter 7

Starting Something You Can't Finish

"What's up, Samuel? It's been a while since we spoke, man. I see that rich ass Pastor life of yours has been keeping you from staying in touch with a brotha. What can I do for ya, pimpin'?" Roy chuckled.

"Naw, man it's not what you think. You've been the big brother I never had. This career of mine is no picnic in the park and I'm in desperate need of a vacation."

"I was only messing witcha, dawg. I know you have to entertain the masses. You know I'm not the kind of man to knock another man's hustle. Shit, at least you're legit. So, how is the missus and the little missus?"

"They're good."

"How about Papa Woodrow?"

"No disrespect, but I'd rather not talk about him right now."

"He still dicking you around, huh?" Roy laughed.

"Like I said, I'd rather not talk about him right now. I'm in no mood for small talk. I need to give you the run down, and then I'm going to need a tall favor from you."

"Go 'head, bruh. I'm all ears."

"I'm a pastor, and as much as I know I'm not supposed to use profane language, I'm ready to let it out today. I have a lot of stuff to get off my chest."

"Bruh, I know it's not easy running a congregation while being scoped out by the media all the damn time. Those muthafuckas forget that celebrities are people too. I'm surprised you haven't spazzed out yet. So, speak your mind; I ain't got nothing but time," Roy said and laughed again.

Samuel inhaled and exhaled. He grabbed his water bottle, drank the remaining drops, and swam into everything that was eating him alive. "Do you remember Sista Rosetta?" he began.

"Yeah, she's the one who marched with Martin Luther King, Jr and shit, right?"

"Right. She passed away last week."

"Say word?" Roy remarked.

"Yep, and you don't want to know where they found her."

"Try me."

"They found her face down in a bowl of tomato soup. Man, I had to hold my laughter in because the shit was too funny."

"Damn, man." Roy's laughed. "Wow, that is some funny ass shit, man."

"Shit, tell me about it," Samuel said while shaking his head.

"So when is the funeral?"

"It will be held on Thursday, but that is not even the biggest problem, though."

"Then what is it then? Because you already know I gotcha back, homie."

The sincerity in Roy's voice gave Samuel a sense of security and he knew he could tell Roy anything. Samuel also knew Roy would do anything for him without question.

"Man, this ugly stank ho waltzed into my office barking orders at me, because I forgot about my appointment with her. Then she told me that she wants me to give Sista Rosetta a fancy funeral. She's the granddaughter of Rosetta. Now get this; she told me that Sista Rosetta left her $75,000 to pay for her funeral expenses, yet she wants me and the church to cover all of the expenses while she flounces her sagging booty ass around in the Bahamas with her boyfriend. And the bitch claims she's married!"

"Daaaammmn, dawg. That's that bullshit right there."

"But that's not all, though."

"Wow. Well, what else did she say?"

"I'm getting to it. The saggy ass having bitch had the niggadacity to hike her skirt up and moon me, and told me to kiss her natural black ass. Then she threatened to have a crooked cop plant drugs on me if I choose not to succumb to her demands."

"What the...are you for real, man? That's really fucked up. So, you want me to take care of that for ya, dawg?"

"Exactly, but I don't want you to kill her, though. You and I both know how ruthless you are. I just want you to pump fear into the bitch—that's all."

"Not a problem, dawg. I gotcha. I'll give you the scoop when I'm done. So, what's her name?"

"Oh yeah, her name is Nadine Burns."

"Cool, do you know where this Nadine bitch lives?"

"No, but I can find out and get back to you."

"Alright."

"Man, that broad has gotten so far under my skin, I can taste it! I wanted to slap her ass pretty. She's so goddamn ugly, she could make an onion cry."

Roy erupted in laughter. "I'm sorry, dawg. What you said is funny as hell," Roy said, on the brink of tears of mirth.

"I'm serious, man. You should have seen her. She can't afford to act ugly when she's ugly on the outside," Samuel remarked and shook his head.

"I understand, dawg, but like I said, I'm gonna take care of that for you. She fucked with the right one. When I get done with her, she's gonna wish the grim reaper had sent her an invitation to his apartment downstairs. Make sure you give me her address and I'll pay the ho a visit," Roy reminded.

"Sure thing, man. I'm going to get on it and I'll hit you up shortly."

"Alright, man. Stay up. Don't let the bullshit get you down, okay?"

"I know, man. I know."

"Well, I got some business to handle. I'll talk to you later. Peace."

"Peace," Samuel said and hung up. He laid back in his chair. He wondered what kind of shady business Roy was up to; whatever it was, it wasn't anything good. Samuel chuckled to himself because he knew if his conservative minions knew he kept company with a miscreant like Roy, they'd come down hard on him like a thunderstorm.

However, Roy was like his big brother and no one understood Samuel better than Roy did. Samuel silently prayed that Roy wouldn't kill Nadine. He knew what Roy was capable of, and he knew he wouldn't be able to live with himself if Roy killed her. Samuel's thoughts deflected from his problems when he powered on his computer. He googled "Constantine" and a list of results came up. Then his office line rang.

"World Faith Missionary Baptist. This is Pastor—"

"Remember what I told you, Pastor Pimp." It was Nadine.

Samuel's anger resurfaced. "What the hell do you want now?"

"Nothing, nigga. I just wanna make sho' you got the message loud and clear. Yo' ass have till Thursday mawnin' to accept my proposition. If not, that's yo' ass. Have a nice day, Pastor Pimp." The line went dead.

Samuel stared at the phone intently and reconsidered calling and asking Roy to finish the job all the way. Samuel knew he could retrieve Nadine's personal records through a good friend named Richie Lee Cobbs. Richie was one of Samuel's few less-conservative church members, who worked as a supervisor at the Department of Motor Vehicles. He was another person Samuel trusted, but not as much as he trusted Roy. Richie was laid-back and straight to the point and he wasn't stiff like most of the church members. He treated Samuel like a man, not God, unlike most of his members. He phoned Richie and he answered on the first ring.

"Hey, brotha man. What's up?" Richie cheerily answered.

"I'm doing okay, bruh. How are you?" Samuel lied.

"I'm livin'. Are you sure you're alright, brotha man, because you don't sound okay," Richie replied in a concerned tone.

Samuel didn't want Richie to know his true motives and why he sounded glum. So, he fed Richie one of his best excuses, hoping Richie would sop it up with some understanding and eat it all up. "No, I'm fine. I'm just a little under the weather, but I'll be okay."

"Alright. Well, how is the family doing?"

"They're fine. We just found out my wife is two months pregnant."

"Really, man? That is fantastic. Congratulations. I was kind of wondering why ya wife had been looking so beautiful lately when I see her. I mean, don't get me wrong; she always looks beautiful. It's just that she has that glow about her. Man, you are one lucky fella. How long do you plan to keep her pregnancy a secret from the congregation," Richie asked with a smile in his voice.

"Thanks, Rich. 'Preciate it, man. We're going to wait until we know the sex of the baby and then we'll announce it to the congregation. You're one of the first ones to know. Promise me you won't tell a soul."

"Now, why would I do that to a well-known televangelist who I consider a blood brotha?" Richie said, pretending he was insulted.

"I was only messing with you, man. You know you're one of the few people I respect," Samuel laughed but he meant well.

"Oh, okay. I was about to say," Richie replied, laughed again and continued, "So, what would you like to have this time?"

"I was hoping for a son, but it really doesn't matter. As long as the baby is healthy, that is what counts."

"Amen to that, brotha man."

Dead silence lingered on the line after he replied.

"I want to ask you a favor," Samuel finally said.

"What's that?" Richie asked as he switched his cell phone to his other ear.

"Do you think you can look someone up for me and give me their address? I believe she's a long-lost cousin of Pauline's and I'd like to get in contact with her."

"Sure, man. What's her name?"

"Her name is Nadine Burns," Samuel uttered.

"Nadine Burns?" Richie repeated

"Yes."

"Hmm…her name sounds familiar."

"Really?" Samuel flinched in horror, but he didn't lead Richie onto it though. He simply played along. "Is she someone you know?"

"I probably know her through a friend or something, but I know that name from somewhere. How do you think Pauline's related to her?" Richie asked and scratched his scraggly beard.

Samuel hadn't expected Richie to ask him that question. Luckily, he was skilled at thinking on his feet. "Yeah, umm, I believe she's my wife's long-lost cousin," Samuel repeated and fidgeted with his cufflinks to calm his nerves from the lie he'd just told twice.

"Really, man? How did ya wife discover that?" Richie excitedly asked.

"She did a genealogical search on her family, and discovered that her cousin was the daughter of her aunt who had her out of wedlock when she was 12 years old. Her mother had to give her up for adoption because her parents, being notably influential in the education system, didn't want their daughter's birth to stain their reputation."

Poor Richie was nodding his head, engrossed in Samuels's story, not knowing that it was all made up. Samuel was surprised with himself because he was equally engulfed in his own lie.

"Wow, that is something else. But do you think it'd be wiser if y'all called her, instead of dropping by her house unannounced?" Richie inquired.

"I agree, but Pauline said she tried to find her on Facebook, LinkedIn, Twitter, and she had no luck. So, she decided it'd be easier for her to contact Nadine in person instead."

"Oh, I see," Richie said with a nod. "Well, you know I'd do anything for ya, brotha man. I'll get on that as soon as I return to work on Monday and send you everything you need."

"Thanks so much, Rich. With Pauline being the prissy conservative she is, she normally wouldn't go for anything like this, but in this case, I know she'd kiss you."

"Well, if it's on the lips, I accept," Richie joked.

"Alright, don't let your tongue get you into something you can't get your behind out of," Samuel laughed, but he was kind of being serious too.

"I'm only playin', brotha man. You know I got nothin' but utmost respect for you and your wife."

"I know, man," Samuel said. He laughed again, but a hint of seriousness remained in his tone. He quickly turned down his seriousness and turned up his cheeriness. "I can't thank you enough, Rich."

"Don't mention it, brotha man. You know I'll always have ya back."

"Cool. Call me up when you find out and we'll talk soon, okay?"

"Alright. Take it easy, brotha man."

"You too." Samuel was relieved and disappointed at the same time, because he hated lying to one of his good friends, who'd probably die for him if he had to.

However, he was relieved to know that he'd be rid of that Nadine character soon...

On the Friday evening of that same week, Nadine sat slouched on her couch watching "Friday" while smoking a blunt and eating pork rinds.

"Ahaha, Smokey, you are one funny ass nigga!" Nadine said. She was watching the scene when Hector and his friend had Smokey running down the street in his white wife beater and underwear, after making him take a toke on some angel dust. There was a knock at the door.

Her loud laughter melded with the loud TV volume, and she didn't hear the knock. The knocks grew louder and louder until she heard a loud thump at the door, which startled her. She immediately turned the volume down.

"Ja'Vontae, is that yo' ass at the do'?" Ja'Vontae was Nadine's boyfriend. He'd went out to order fried pork ribs, potato salad, collard greens, and generic beer earlier.

"No, ma'am. This is Detective Ernie Frye."

Nadine's eyes changed from slits to wide open and her heart galloped like a greyhound in a race. She mentally rewound back to any of her wrongdoings, but her marijuana laced psyche wouldn't give her a helping hand. Then the sight of the scattered remnants of hash on her coffee table brought her back to her senses again.

"Just a minute," she shouted at the door.

She hastily collected the weed, scooped it into a Ziploc bag with her bare hands, sealed it shut, and shoved it under the sofa.

"I'm coming," she said nervously and ran into the bathroom to grab the can of air freshener. When she returned to the living room, she saturated the room with it to smother the marijuana smoke.

"Lawd, I hope this pig don't see the red in my eyes from all the weed I smoked," she mumbled to herself. Never mind the fact that her hair resembled wild grass and her white tank top and hot pink mini shorts were speckled with fish grease stains. Nadine carefully looked through the peep hole and saw another eye looking straight into hers. She immediately jumped back.

"Whatchu want?" she huffily asked, but on the down low, she was scared to death.

"Ma'am, I cannot speak with you through the door. I'm going to need you to open the door, please."

Nadine took a deep breath and obliged. She opened the door, but she kept the chain on. "Is there a problem, Officer?" she carefully asked through the narrow space.

"Ma'am, my name is Detective Ernie Frye," he said and showed her his badge. "Are you Nadine Burns?"

"Yes I am, Officer," Nadine said in a shaky voice.

"Are you related to Rosetta Madison?"

"Yes, sir."

"Mind if I come in?"

"No, I don't mind, Officer; wait a minute." Nadine nervously closed the door, unhooked the chain, and reopened it for him to come in.

"Thank you, Mrs. Burns," he said as he entered the house.

"Would you like to have a seat, Officer?"

"No, I'm fine. This will only be a few minutes."

"Oh, okay. Ummm, would you like somethin' to drank? Some soda, water, orange juice befo' we talk?" Nadine offered while nervously wringing her wrists.

"Sure, I'll have a glass of soda, please," the officer said casually.

"Alright, I'll be right back," Nadine said and raced to the kitchen.

The officer heard her mumbling under her breath in the kitchen, but he didn't know what she was talking about. He shrugged it off. Then he pulled out his gun, cocked it, and aimed it in the direction of the kitchen.

"Here's yo' drank of—" she stopped short when she saw the gun. Nadine dropped the glass of soda and the glass splattered on her wooden floor, cutting up her legs and scarring her floor. She was too shocked to feel the pain. "What the…"

"What's the matter, bitch? Cat gotcha tongue," he asked as he stepped closer to Nadine with the gun still pointed at her forehead.

"What is goin' on?" Nadine sobbed while holding her hands up to shield herself from the gun.

"I want you to bring your ass over here and sit down." He grabbed her by her arm and shoved her into the recliner chair. He kept the gun aimed at her head. By then, Nadine's face was drenched in tears.

"Please don't hurt me," she begged and wiped the blood from her legs.

"Shut up, bitch," he barked and slapped her. Nadine was bawling like a baby. "I said shut the hell up!" he barked again and pointed the gun at her temple. Nadine immediately stopped crying, but she was shaking like an overheated car. "I want you to listen to something," he said and kept the gun pointed at Nadine's head as he pulled out his cell phone, dialed a number and turned on the speakerphone.

Samuel answered on the second ring. "What's up, Roy?"

"What's up, homie? Guess where I am?" There was a pregnant pause. "Samuel, are you there?"

"Umm, yeah, I'm here. Are you with someone?" Samuel cautiously asked; he didn't want to believe Roy was at Nadine's house.

"I'm not at just anyone's house. I'm at this bitch Nadine's house. Hey, man; I got her ass at gunpoint as we speak," Roy snickered.

"What? Roy, what the hell is wrong with you—" Samuel stopped short and tried to unscramble his thoughts for a second. "Take me off speakerphone, now!" he demanded.

"Aw, come on, Samuel. You told me you wanted me to handle this for ya, right?"

"Roy, I don't feel comfortable discussing this over the speakerphone," Samuel cautiously said. Samuel's heart was running laps in his chest and he was sweating so profusely, his sweat was sweating. He knew Roy had committed acts that made God gasp, but he didn't think Roy would put him on the spot in front of Nadine, of all people. "Please, Roy," Samuel begged, "take me off the speakerphone so we can talk in private."

"You bitch ass niggas ain't gon' get away with this shit!" Nadine screamed in terror.

"Bitch, didn't I tell you shut the hell up!" Roy knocked Nadine across the face with the butt of his gun, causing blood to hurl out of her mouth. Nadine was petrified and she continued to cry terribly. "See, this is what I hate about you loudmouth, ghetto bitches. And you wonder why we kill bitches like you and do long bids and shit. Samuel, you should let me cancel this bitch like an order of condoms, dawg.

There are no other witnesses except you and me!" Roy fumed while waving the gun around in the air.

Samuel was shocked and his tongue was experiencing paralysis. He had to swallow hard to reactivate his tongue. He knew when Roy was mad it was hard to calm him down.

Samuel recalled when he and Roy had met for lunch at a five-star seafood restaurant; one of the waitresses had acted like she didn't want to tend to their table. He and Samuel had already waited an hour for a table, and when they were finally seated, they'd had to wait an additional ten minutes to be serviced. When Roy asked the waitress for a menu, she'd ignored him and assisted other customers who hadn't waited as long as he and Samuel had. Those customers were white, and ironically the waitress was black. When the waitress ignored him, Roy's eyes turned to fire and brimstone, and he approached the waitress; when she turned around, he punched her so hard, she fell onto the customers she was helping and they all went tumbling down like dominoes. Roy simply turned and trudged out of the restaurant as if nothing had happened. Samuel had been so embarrassed, he'd asked the waitress if she was okay. It was a good thing he'd chosen to disguise himself in a dreadlock wig, baseball cap, and sunglasses, because he would've ended up on the front cover of tabloid magazines otherwise. And that was the last time he'd gone anywhere with Roy.

"Listen, Roy. I don't want you to kill her, man. She isn't worth it."

"Oh, so now you punkin' out like a lil bitch?" Roy questioned with an incredulous look.

"That's not it, man! If you kill her, we'll both have her blood on our hands!"

"What the hell are you talking about? You're not the one with the gun, and after I kill this ho we'll still go on with our respective lives!"

"I understand, but you have to remember; I am a man of the cloth, and God isn't going to like this one bit. I never told you to kill her, but if you do, we're both going to be accountable, because I gave you permission to go to her house. It's like I'm standing next to you!"

"Oh, so now you actin' all brand new since I told you I'm about to off this bitch because you're afraid of losing your goddamn career and scared of what God is going to do to you? I can't believe you, dawg." Roy burst into laughter.

Samuel wasn't amused at all. He had never felt so uneasy in all of his days. He didn't care about Nadine, but he wouldn't be able to live with the fact of her being murdered either.

Roy resumed his tirade. "This ho disrespected and threatened you, and now you catch feelings for her and shit," he ranted as he waved his gun around like a mad serial killer.

"That's not what this is all about, dammit! Didn't you ever stop to think that I have a family to support? If you kill this woman, my life, career, and freedom will be over!" Samuel boomed and slammed his fist on the desk.

"You know what? Screw it. One of us has to have the balls, and it's going to be me—as usual," Roy replied.

"Roy, don't do it. Roy—"

Pow! Pow! Pow!

The line went dead. Samuel frantically redialed Roy's number repeatedly, but it went to voicemail every time. "Fuuuuuuuuuuck!" Samuel yelled.

Chapter 8

News Blues

Samuel was a mixture of emotions. He was so out of it, he looked like a zombie, and his body felt like a heavy log. He needed a strong stiff drink.

"Daddy, Daddy!" Chastity ran up to Samuel, hopped into his arms, and gave him a big kiss on the cheek. "I missed you, Daddy," she said with the biggest smile on her adorable face.

"I missed you too, pumpkin, but right now Daddy needs some rest, okay?" Chastity nodded and Samuel gently put her down.

"Hi, honey. How was your day?" Pauline greeted Samuel with open arms. When she tried to kiss him, he turned his face the other way and gently shoved her away.

"Please; not now, Pauline." He peeled his jacket off and placed it on the coat hanger.

Pauline furrowed her eyebrows in disbelief. "What's wrong, Samuel?"

"It's nothing. I just had a long day, that's all," Samuel said without looking at Pauline. He walked straight to the kitchen to pour himself a glass of vodka.

Pauline followed him into the kitchen. "Samuel, if something is bothering you, you should talk about it. You preach about communication in the marriage all the time in church. If there's something bothering you, you—"

"Sweetheart, I know what I said, okay? But right now, I need some time to think. We'll talk about it later, alright?" Samuel lied. Samuel knew he would never tell Pauline what was bothering him because he had no intentions of telling her about the horrible incident that had occurred earlier.

Pauline gave him another puzzled look. "Baby, you shouldn't be drinking before dinner. It's going to ruin your appetite," she remarked.

"I'm not hungry," Samuel said and filled the glass all the way to the rim.

"Whatever is bothering you, we can fix it," she said with pleading eyes.

Samuel took long gulps of his drink and burped. Pauline grimaced at him. Samuel tried to pour himself another helping, but Pauline intervened.

"Baby, don't you think you've had enough?" Pauline softly asked as she tried to take the bottle out of his hand.

"Woman, I am a grown ass man. I don't need you telling me when I've had enough of anything," he spat and violently pulled away from her.

Pauline's eyes began to glisten. "Samuel, what has gotten into you? It's like—"

"Goddamn, Pauline. Which part of, 'I need some time to think' do you not understand?! You know what? My father is right; you women don't know how to let a man be a man and shut the fuck up!" Samuel venomously remarked.

Pauline gasped and covered her mouth. The tears started sprinkling out of her eyes and she shook her head. "What have I ever done to you for you to treat me this way?" she sobbed.

Samuel stepped closer to Pauline, grabbed her chin and forced her eyes to meet his. "Don't you mean, what have I ever done for you?"

Pauline tried to pry his hands off her chin and look away, but Samuel gripped her chin tighter and continued to make her look into his eyes. "I've bought you everything you've ever dreamed of. I bought you a ten million dollar house, a BMW, and jewelry from Tiffany's. I take you out on exotic trips, buy you designer clothes, and most of all, I gave you a beautiful child, including the one you're carrying. If it wasn't for me, you'd be another broke ass college dropout. I am Pastor Samuel goddamn Lee Baker, and don't you ever forget that." Samuel released his grip on her chin and grabbed the vodka bottle.

Pauline's face was flooded with tears and she cupped her face and sobbed uncontrollably. Samuel opened the vodka bottle again. "Cheers to ungrateful ass wives," he said, held his drink high, then gulped the alcohol greedily. "I'm going to go watch television. Clean your face before Chastity comes in and finds you weeping like a big ass baby," he said with disgust, and exited the kitchen.

When he reentered the living room, Chastity was lying in front of the TV, coloring in her book. She was very smart for her age, so she was wise enough to know when her father needed some time alone.

If only Pauline knew how to take a damn hint like Chastity, I wouldn't have to raise my damn voice, he thought.

He could still hear the gun shots in his head. And if that wasn't harrowing enough, the six o'clock news spread across his humongous flat screen TV at that moment.

The newscaster stared into the camera solemnly and said, "We have breaking news. Thirty-three-year old Nadine Burns was brutally murdered in Liberty City on 79th Avenue tonight. Her boyfriend, Ja'Vontae Simmons, found her slumped on her sofa with three gunshot wounds—two in her head and one in her chest. Her boyfriend isn't the suspect in this matter, but he is being questioned by police. Police are still investigating. We'll have more developing news at ten. I am Mitch Camp, reporting to you live from Channel Six."

Samuel's facial expression and body froze. He stared blankly at the TV screen, trying to register Nadine's reported death. His throat was so tight, he couldn't swallow, and his palms were sweaty. He sat there like a mannequin until his daughter stood up in front of him, and waved her hand in his face to snap him out of his daze.

"Daddy... Daddy? Daddy, say something," Chastity said.

Samuel blinked his eyes and answered her. "Huh? Oh, um, yeah Chastity, what happened?"

Chastity gave Samuel a confounded look. "Daddy, are you okay?"

"Oh, yeah, um, Daddy's fine, pumpkin."

"Are you sure, because I kept talking to you and you said nothing," she wailed while tilting her head to the side.

"Aww, pumpkin, come here." Samuel picked Chastity up and placed her on his lap. "Daddy is sorry for ignoring you. It's just that I've been working very hard so that you and your mommy can have nice things."

Chastity gave Samuel a piercing look. "Daddy?"

"Yes, pumpkin."

"Are you and Mommy getting a divorce?"

"What? Where on earth did you get that idea?"

"Well, you and Mommy always look like you're mad at each other and Mommy always looks sad. I heard you two arguing in the kitchen."

103

Samuel's heart felt like it was lodged in his throat and he swallowed hard to get rid of the sensation. He'd had no idea how observant Chastity was. "Sweetheart, your mother and I love each other very much, and when two people love each other, they have disagreements sometimes. I promise you that your mother and I aren't getting a divorce. We love you very much and you have absolutely nothing to worry about."

"Do you really promise?" Chastity asked with a hint of concern in her tiny voice.

"Of course I do." Samuel gently pinched her nose and tickled her, causing her to erupt in giggles.

"Stop, Daddy. I'm ticklish," she said and continued giggling.

Samuel gave her a kiss on the nose. "Are you excited about becoming a big sister?" he asked.

"Yeaaaaaaaah!" Chastity shouted and Samuel laughed.

"You're going to be a great big sister."

"Yep, and I'm going to the best big sister in the whole wide world!" she boasted.

"I know you are, pumpkin, and I love you very much." Samuel planted a kiss on Chastity's cheek.

"I love you too, Daddy." Chastity gave him a huge bear hug around his neck.

Samuel was torn up on the inside, because he knew he didn't deserve Chastity's affection, not after what had taken place earlier. He quickly removed her arms from his neck and looked her straight in the eyes. "And Daddy apologizes about what happened earlier in the kitchen too, okay?"

Chastity nodded her head approvingly.

"Alright, sweetheart, I'm about to go upstairs and take a nap. You stay here and continue coloring in your book."

Samuel picked up his vodka bottle and peeled himself from the couch. When he approached the staircase, he saw Pauline coming out of the kitchen, and she shot him a defeated look from her bloodshot eyes. They exchanged glares for a few seconds, but didn't say anything. He continued up the stairs to the bathroom and as he trudged along, he guzzled the vodka until only half remained. He entered the bathroom and flopped on the toilet.

He kept hearing Roy's voice and the gun shots echoing in his head. "Stop it," he said while covering his ears. He thought he was going crazy. He continued drinking to drown out the noise in his head, and drool began to run down his chin. By then, he was on his knees, and crawling on the bathroom floor like a baby.

"You're very pathetic!" He heard a voice say. The voice caught him off guard.

"God, is that you?" he whimpered.

"No, fool," the voice responded.

"Well, then it must be the vodka," Samuel said as he drank more of it.

"You're a nigga clown!"

"Yo, who the hell you think you're talking to?" Samuel angrily replied in a drunken slur.

"I mean, just look at you. It's no wonder the devil kicks back and laughs at you. You're a poor excuse for a black man and your shortcomings are waiting for you around the corner. If you don't hurry up and face your truth, you'll be sorry," the voice reprimanded.

"Argh, whatever; my life is already over," Samuel dismissively waved and sucked on the vodka bottle like an infant.

"Get up from the floor and look at me!" the voice demanded powerfully.

Samuel slowly stood up against the wall and looked aimlessly around the bathroom. He burped so fiercely, the bathroom door shook a little. Once again, he looked at the mirror and stared his future self in the face.

"What do you want from me?" Samuel asked with frustration as he leaned in to get a closer look at his future image.

His eyes were red from all the vodka he'd consumed and the dark circles around his eyes verified that he had a sleep deficit.

"You have gone astray, and you're leading your flock astray too. You should repent for what happened to that woman and you must begin shedding your old self for your new self. Brother, you are your own worst foe and the only one who can help you become a new you is the Messiah and the Father. But before you get to know them, you must be truthful to yourself," his reflection revealed.

107

"And how do I do that? I had a woman killed because I was afraid she would have me framed for drugs that weren't mine; my best friend Roy is nowhere to be found, and he's just as guilty for her murder as I am. How am I supposed to undo that?" Samuel helplessly asked as he desperately searched the face of his future self for answers.

"Roy is not your friend, and you need to cut him off. He is a dangerous thug who will perish, and if you keep befriending him, you're going to perish with him. You're an accomplice to a murder you didn't commit and now you have two choices; you can tell the police what you did and go down with that joker and become another number in the system, or you can implore the Most High for redemption and fast to cleanse yourself of all of your iniquities."

Samuel began crying and the saliva and mucus that left his mouth and nose made him look like he had placenta on his face—minus the blood. As he wept, one of his nostrils grew a snot bubble and it popped.

"Stop crying like a girl and lift your nuts! This is no time for emotionalism. We are in the end times and when it all hits the fan, you'll be accountable for everything you do. It is time to face the music, boy," his future image authoritatively said and pointed his finger so far at Samuel, the finger nearly touched his nose.

Samuel looked at the index finger and went cross-eyed for a second. Then he looked at his future self and stepped back a few inches. "How am I supposed to make this right?" Samuel asked in bewilderment.

His future image shook his head and laughed. He replied in a bitter voice, "You're a church pimp and a national con artist, yet you ask how do you make this right? You need to look at your Bible and read it from Genesis to Revelation. Then, you need to turn to your good friend, Richie. That brother is the only man who can save you from your pathetic self."

"Richie?" Samuel asked in surprise. "How will he able to save me from myself?"

"You have everything you need, but you're too damn stupid to see it. This truth isn't for everyone, and when you discover and understand it for yourself, you will become a foreigner in your own matrix," his future image said in an instructive tone.

"But what about the girl?" Samuel uncertainly asked.

"I've already given you two solutions. You can do it the easy way or the hard way. I hope you make the right decision and go in the right path. Once you do that, I will merge with you and we'll collide with iniquity. I've spoken my piece for now and I shall return at a later time. Shalom, brother."

Samuel's future image disappeared again and Samuel looked pathetically dumbfounded. His trademark lustrous processed hair was now dry, wild, and brittle. His five o'clock shadow had sprouted in and his eyes were sunken.

"I am talking to myself in the mirror. I feel like I'm going crazy. I need to get myself together," he said aloud to himself.

Then he heard a voice in his head. You're not going crazy. You're just losing yourself in this sick twisted Babylonian world. All you have to do is turn away from it, said the voice.

"Stop it! I said stop it, goddamn it." Samuel shook his head and gripped it tight, then he started washing his face.

"Is everything alright in there," Pauline asked from the other side of the door.

Samuel was breathless and he didn't know whether he was going or coming. "Yeah, everything is alright," he replied in an unconvincing tone.

"Samuel, baby, we really need to talk. Baby, can you please open the door?" she gently asked.

Samuel stared at the door and contemplated whether he should let her in or not. He finally opened the door.

Pauline looked at him with those same pleading eyes. Her eyes and nose were red and her face was flushed. "Samuel, I am very worried about you. I really am. I don't know what's become of you. You never drink and use street language, especially not in this house or at me. It's like one minute you're Samuel, and the next minute you're somebody else. For Christ's sake, I can't continue going on like this, and this isn't good for the baby." Pauline looked at her growing belly and began rubbing it as she started to weep silently.

Samuel sighed and ran his fingers through his disheveled hair. "Sweetheart, I am very sorry," he said and grabbed her hand and hugged her.

Pauline cried in his arms then stepped back and looked into his eyes. "We need to see a marriage counselor," she stated.

Samuel gave her a perplexed look. "Marriage counselor? What for? I'm a marriage counselor. That is what I do," Samuel defensively said and stood away from her. His sobriety sat in at her suggestion; he wasn't drunk anymore.

"I know, but it would be better if someone from the outside counseled us," she said.

Samuel wasn't the kind of man who sought counseling from anyone because he didn't believe that his shortcomings were anything he couldn't repair. He almost felt insulted by Pauline's suggestion. "Someone, like who?" he asked, sounding miffed.

"Well, Bridgette Brice would be an ideal counselor. She's a reverend, licensed psychologist; and she's authored three New York Times Bestselling self-help books. I think she's more than qualified," Pauline explained.

Samuel's temper was getting hot and if it got any hotter, he'd spit fire and burn the entire house down. "Yeah, she's qualified alright; she's a certified KKK, man-bashing, God-despising, lesbian witch! And she only caters to white women because she hates the fact that she's half-black! Jesus Christ, woman. Have you gone mad?" Samuel huffily remarked.

"Sssshh, can you lower your voice? Chastity can hear you," Pauline complained. "And besides, the woman was raped when she was five years old. She's all about empowering women of all races and nationalities; not once has she ever stated that she hates black people."

"No, but her actions say it. Look, I don't want to hear any more of this rubbish," Samuel said and gently walked around Pauline, exited the bathroom and headed to the bedroom.

Pauline followed suit. When Samuel entered the bedroom, he walked to the bed, sat on it and began removing his shoes and tie. "Either we get counseling, or our marriage is going to crumble," Pauline continued. "Bridgette is a lesbian, but it doesn't deflect from her being a remarkable, God-fearing womanist and philanthropist. She's donated hundreds and thousands of dollars to several charities, and she's been on Oprah's show three times. We can definitely afford her services, and I really think she'd be a great aspect to saving our marriage. Please, baby, just give it some thought." Pauline sat next to Samuel and put her arms around his shoulders.

He vehemently got up and stood in front of her. "Now I know you've really lost your mind or you've been reading one of her books. I'm all too familiar with her story and I know what she's all about. Bridgette Brice is a money-hungry reprobate; she pimps white women and she hates black men the way Oprah does. I'm not condoning what happened to her as a child, because no human being deserves that. But you've forgotten that she recently made an announcement to her congregation about getting a sex change; all because she was raped by her own sick, black grandfather. She hates her black blood and she only loves her white counterparts because of it. Now, if that isn't sick foolery, I don't know what is!" Samuel angrily said and walked to the dresser drawer to collect his pajamas.

"Yes, I am well aware of all of it, but she is more than her past. She is an influential human being and I know she has a personal relationship with God. She's biracial, gay, and she wants to become a man…so what? Only God can judge her, not you," Pauline exclaimed and folded her arms.

Samuel swung his neck around and shot Pauline a look that was so evil, Lucifer would have ducked for cover. "So you're saying it's okay for people of the same gender to have sex, right?"

"No, but the way people choose to live their lives isn't any of our business, and it isn't harming us. I mean, you and I aren't perfect. So, who are we to judge anyway?"

"Okay, so…as long as other people commit incest, murder, have sex with animals, rape, steal, lie, cheat, fornicate and commit adultery, that makes it okay, too?" Samuel pointed out.

"Absolutely not! Those aren't the same as homosexuality and you're trying to shove words in my mouth. Homosexuals share the same love as heterosexuals. And you and I both know that love has no color or gender. It is pure, harmless, and sacred, and God loves us all, no matter what," Pauline defensively said.

"Oh, so you're twisting God's words now? Forget about what he did to Sodom and Gomorrah and Lot's wife. Leviticus 20: 13 says, 'If a man also lie with mankind, as he lieth with a woman: both of them have committed an abomination: they shall surely be put to death; their blood shall be upon them'," Samuel recited.

Pauline dismissively waved her hand. "I know the scriptures, Samuel. We're not in church—"

"No, you just listen and say nothing. Since you condone wickedness, I want you to listen well because listening is your greatest weakness. God said to Moses in Leviticus 18:22, 'Thou shalt not lie with mankind as with womankind: it is abomination.' In Ezekiel 20:7 'Then I said unto them, Cast ye away every man the abominations of his eyes, and defile not yourselves with the idols of Egypt: I am the Lord your God. But they rebelled against me, and would not hearken unto me: they did not every man cast away the abominations of their eyes, neither did they forsake the idols of Egypt: then I said, I will pour out my fury upon them, to accomplish my anger against them in the midst of the land of Egypt.' I can go on and on, but I'll stop there." Samuel looked Pauline up and down in pure disgust. "You have no idea how abominable you sound, and I'd rather not sleep in the same bed with you. Until you repent about the things you said, I will sleep in the guest room," Samuel added as he returned to the chest of drawers and closed the drawer.

Pauline was on the brink of tears again but she didn't let them fall. "Samuel, why can't you understand those were the times then, not now? Times have changed and people are free to love whoever they want," Pauline said and tried to follow Samuel again.

Samuel gave her the most dirtiest look she'd ever seen and she stepped back because she was afraid he may strike her again. "I think you'd better leave because my thoughts are dying to come out of my mouth, and if you aren't out of this room within three seconds, I won't be able to recant anything I say, nor will I regret it," he threatened and stepped closer to her.

"Fine," she finally said and hurriedly went to the door. But before she stepped out of the room, she gave Samuel one good hard look. "I really love you, Samuel and I want our marriage to work for Chastity's and our unborn child's sake. I am willing to do whatever I can to make it work. I hope you understand," she sadly said and left.

Samuel bit his tongue to prevent it from lashing out at Pauline. *Sometimes I don't even understand people. Roy kills Nadine against my will and now Pauline's telling me that homosexuality is okay and that we should seek professional marriage counseling from some reprobate ass lesbian who is on the cusp of getting a sex change. Folks are losing their goddamn minds and if I don't find some answers, I am going explode like dynamites in lava!* Samuel thought.

He got on his knees and began saying a prayer. "Dear Lord, I am losing my mind. One of my dearest friends, Roy, killed Nadine Burns; my marriage has cracks in it, and my wife wants me to see a lesbian marriage counselor who has her lick hers license. Lord, I need answers and I am afraid I am going to hurt somebody! I feel like my mind is playing games with me, and I'm slowly falling out of love with the church and being a deceiver. Am I wrong for feeling this way? What am I supposed to do when the entire world depends on me to be truthful, when I don't feel that way on the inside? Please, Lord, you must help me. I am sick of this crap and I'm tired of being the nice guy. I don't endorse homosexuality and all these other iniquities, but I am sucking the money out of my congregation. If you don't help me, I won't be sorry for what I do. In Jesus' name...Amen."

Chapter 9

Funeral Foolery

That Monday morning arrived in a flash, and it was the most dreadful day of Samuel's life. He had to preside over Sista Rosetta's wake that day, and her funeral on Thursday, but he just was in no mood for church. He felt pretty awkward because her granddaughter Nadine was dead and police were still investigating her death, but he still hadn't heard from Roy.

He and Pauline weren't speaking and the tension between them was thicker than syrup. Pauline slept in her bed while he slept in the guest room; he had nightmares about that horrible incident with Nadine each time he fell asleep, and he woke up in cold sweats. When awake, Samuel had out-of-body experiences and he continued to have flashbacks about that horrible incident.

Rosetta's family showed up for the wake, and their moods matched their black attire. He had put out the memo for her wake and funeral days ago, and nearly

119

the entire neighborhood had shown up today for her wake. Rosetta's estranged children, Ashley and Benjamin also showed up.

Ashley was tall, skinny, light skinned, and the freckles on her face were so tiny, they appeared to dance around her face like tiny black ants. She looked like she probably favored her father, who'd died from a heart attack when she was a junior in high school, because she bore no resemblance to Rosetta. She wore a black wool dress that stopped at her knees and her hair was pulled back into a bun, bringing out her doe-like eyes and expanding her regal aura. She was a natural beauty.

Her younger brother, Benjamin on the other hand, was the darker version and he looked like Rosetta. He was short and stocky like a Build-A-Bear, and he wore a paisley shirt with brown plaid pants, making him look like Mr. Brown from "Meet the Browns." One of the buttons on his shirt hung from a thread and the shirt looked like it was struggling to accommodate his pudgy frame. As Samuel shook hands with the incoming crowd, Benjamin approached.

"How are you today, Pastor Baker?" Benjamin said with a wide smile, zealously shaking Samuel's hand. Samuel twisted his lips at Benjamin because he'd wiped his forehead with his paw-like hand first, then proceeded to shake Samuel's hand with it. Benjamin's hand was greasy and it smelled like booty.

"I am doing fine," Samuel said with a pseudo smile. "I am really sorry about your mother Rosetta," he continued without looking Benjamin in the eyes.

"Thanks, man. But now that she is gone, I can finally buy that Ferrari I always wanted," he said with a toothy grin.

"I beg your pardon," Samuel said with a bewildered expression and looked Benjamin up and down.

"My mama was a fine gal, but she had money. She ain't never wanna give me no money for nothin', but now that she dead, I'm finally gonna be able to start my clothing line," Benjamin said with pride on his face.

Samuel was beyond disgusted that a man who looked like he shopped out of the dumpster would speak about initiating a fashion line. Let alone speak about how he was going to spend his mother's money after she'd just passed away. Not once did he mention anything about covering the funeral expenses or memorializing her.

The niggadacity of some folks. This rhino's clothes are so tight, his balls and nipples are probably gasping for air. I guess it runs in the family, because none of Rosetta's so-called family seems to give a cat's ass about her, Samuel thought. Although he didn't care for Rosetta, he still had enough respect to defend her legacy in public. "You are in the Lord's house, and I know he isn't pleased with your inappropriate behavior or attitude; neither am I," Samuel said matter-of-factly.

"Oh, lighten up, Pastor. Even the Lord has a sense of humor," Benjamin said with a chuckle.

"There is a time and a place for everything," Samuel irritatingly said and shot Benjamin a lethal look that could have put him in a coffin too.

"Calm down, Pastor. I was only joking. Besides, Mama wouldn't have minded one lil bit. She always said the Lord told jokes to the angels," Benjamin nervously said for the sake of not getting his head chewed off by Samuel.

"I see you haven't wasted any time charming the man, huh, Benjamin?" Ashley said in her sadity voice.

"Naw, it's all good. Ain't that right, Pastor?" Benjamin said and attempted to give Samuel a high five.

"Ahem, um…I am very, um…sorry about your mom and daughter, Ms. Ashley," Samuel said. He cleared his throat, looked to the floor, and ignored Benjamin while shifting his weight from one side to the other.

"Now, now, Pastor Baker; my mother was a wonderful woman and she did a lot for the black community, but she was no saint either. She was…" Ashley's eyes and voice trailed off as she batted her eyes and tried to keep her tears hostage. And then she continued, "My mother was a trashy black wench and I'm glad she's dead. I guess that's where my daughter, Nadine, got it from. It explains why we were estranged. She was such a hood rat floozy, always defending my no-good ass mammy. Great, now they both can join each other in hell," Ashley revealed, pulled out her fingernail file and began filing her nails.

Samuel gasped so hard, he went cross-eyed. Ashley had piqued Samuel's curiosity when she'd called her mother a trashy black wench. And what was worse, she showed no emotion about her own daughter being deceased. "Ms. Ashley, how can you say those callous things about your daughter and mother? They were far from perfect, but they were still your family," Samuel said matter-of-factly with a twinge of guilt.

"But she's right," Benjamin chimed in. "Mama was never no saint. She used to make us watch her have sex with married couples while Papa was at work and she would force Ashley here to go down on they husbands. I had my first piece of coochie when I was five years old. Mama forced me to stick my dang-a-lang in—"

"Benjamin!" Ashley shot him a nasty and bewildered look. "Why do you have to bring all that up?" she shouted and threw her nail file back inside of her purse. "Can you just keep your pig feet sucking mouth shut for once?" Ashley scolded and slapped her right hand against her hip.

Benjamin was unfazed and chuckled a little. "How long do you think you can carry around a secret that don' put you on that bull daggin' white woman's loony couch? What's her name again? Umm…" Benjamin said while pensively looking in the air like he was trying to figure out a difficult Algebra equation.

That's when Ashley lost her composure. "It's Bridgette Brice, you illiterate 8th grade drop-out! And for your pathetic information, Bridgette Brice is mulatto, not WHITE! But I suppose you wouldn't know what mulatto is because you can barely write your own name. Ugh! Sometimes I wish I was white because I can't stand niggers. Especially stupid ones like you," Ashley huffed and stormed off.

This time Samuel was too outdone and if nothing else was going to make him think negatively about church, the showdown between Ashley and Benjamin was. In fact, he was secretly enjoying it. Some of the church members were beginning to notice the unfolding melee.

"Yeah, well I ain't the smartest man in the world, but at least I ain't catch gonorrhea in my mouth from sucking Mr. Thornsby's shriveled up old pecker when I was 10 years old. You can get all the nose jobs, lighten yo' skin, and straighten yo' hair to look like white folks all you want to, but the hair on yo' coochie is still mo' nappy than a camel's ass in Saudi Arabia," Benjamin scoffed with a satisfied smirk on his face.

The rest of the church members gasped in utter shock. Ashley began crying and her lips trembled. "I wish you were dead like our sorry mammy and Nadine. And if it wasn't against the law, I'd hang you from a tree, set your body on fire, and watch you burn to ashes. And black people wonder why I am ashamed of being black!" Ashley shouted and stormed out of the church. "Get the hell out of my way," she barked as she struggled through the crowd of visitors.

She bumped into Meesha Simpson, who looked like she was a chocolate chip cookie away from exploding, and the obese woman tossed in her unsolicited two cents. "Your mama would be very proud of you. You need Jesus!" Meesha said while munching on a family size bag of Doritos.

Ashley glared at Meesha and replied, "And you need Jenny Craig." She continued out of the church, inciting the crowd's emotions.

"Whatever, honey! At least I got Jesus," Meesha proudly said and popped another chip into her mouth.

"Amen to that, sister," the other congregants said.

Benjamin still had a smirk on his face. Samuel looked at him and shook his head. "Aren't you going to go out there to talk to her? It's obvious that your relationship is fractured and there is a huge elephantine gap between you. Your mother and niece wouldn't want you guys acting like this," Samuel said.

"I ain't stuttin' that ol' stuck up heifer. It's about time somebody put her in her place because she likes walkin' round thinkin' she better than everybody. Her milk ain't cleaner than nobody's. She got as much fault as the next person. I could care less 'bout her bein' mad; it ain't like she give a damn 'bout nobody anyway. She don't wanna see nobody happy 'cept herself. I don't need her and I damn sho' don't need nobody else. Well, anyway, I'm hungry. Do you have anything to eat, Pastor? I sho' is hungry," Benjamin said while rubbing his growling stomach like he was in a restaurant rather than a church. "Let me get some of them chips, girl," Benjamin said to Meesha.

"Honey, I'm not giving you anything. I haven't eaten in the past twenty minutes. You should have eaten before you got here," Meesha reprimanded and continued chumping on her Doritos.

"Fine, be that way. I'm 'bout to go order me a pig ear sandwich, French fries, and a large sweet tea at Roscoe's Rib Shack anyway. See y'all later," Benjamin said and headed toward the door where the ushers were standing.

"But what about your mother's wake," Samuel asked with concern on his face.

"If she's dead now, she'll still be dead when I get back," Benjamin nonchalantly said and exited the church.

The congregation was having a gasp fest. They were beyond appalled.

"Pastor, aren't you going to do something?" asked Nina, who burst onto the scene out of nowhere.

Samuel felt like he had egg on his face and he didn't know where to begin. His temples were throbbing so hard, he felt like a donkey had kicked him in his head. It wasn't because of what had happened, but because he really didn't want to be there. "Settle down, folks. I am very sorry about what just happened, but I assure you we're not going to allow what just happened to put a damper on our beloved sister's wake," Samuel said with an extra boost of false assurance.

Pauline finally appeared next to Samuel and she looked like she wanted to die on the scene. Poor Chastity had seen and heard everything and she looked completely confused.

Samuel was beyond embarrassed, so he knelt down before her and apologized. "Sweetheart, I am very sorry you had to hear and see that. Please forgive what you've heard and seen, okay?" he said while chucking her under the chin.

"Daddy, what's gonorrhea and pecker?" Chastity meekly questioned with more confusion on her face.

"Lord have mercy," said Ms. Jessie, who was the second oldest member in the church; then she fainted.

"Oh, my lord," said Nina who rushed to her aid. All of the other members began to swarm around Ms. Jessie.

"Pauline, please take Chastity to the back and keep her in there. She's gotten more than an earful," Samuel frantically instructed.

"I agree with you, dear. Come on, sweetie. I am about to take you to Daddy's office," Pauline said, grabbed Chastity's tiny hand and guided her to the back of the church. It was the first time she and Samuel had spoken since their argument.

"Is she okay?" Samuel asked and began making his way through the crowd. Monroe Bullock, who was also a member and paramedic, came to Jessie's aid and checked her pulse.

Is she going to be alright?" Meesha asked with a mouth full of food.

"I don't think so. She's dead," Monroe said with such a sorrowful look on his face, it would've made a Happy Meal sad.

"Oh, sweet Jesus!" Nina said with her hand over her mouth.

Samuel went and stood next to her to comfort her. "Call the ambulance, Monroe," Samuel ordered.

The crowd was shocked and their emotions were racing like a lizard.

"I'm already on it," Monroe said as he removed his cell phone from his suit jacket pocket and began dialing 9-1-1.

This is just great! Now, I have to preside over another old hag's funeral. Father, please forgive me for the thoughts I cannot tame, Samuel thought. He retreated to the pulpit and picked up his microphone. "I'm going to need all of you to calm down and sit down now!" Samuel yelled and stared angrily at the crowd.

"But what about Sister Jessie?" asked one of the congregants who looked like he was 30 years late for a dental appointment.

"Brother Monroe has it all under control. Just step aside. The ambulance will arrive any second now," Samuel said. Samuel was hoping that no one else would pass out in the church. The chaos was overwhelming and Samuel's headache was drumming so hard, it sounded like a thunderstorm in his ears.

That's when Woodrow graced the scene with his presence. "What the hell is going on," he shouted as he walked between the ushers and streams of people who were trying to take their seats. Poor Rosetta's casket was located in front of the church. She looked like a wax figure; the mortician had applied too much make up.

Pauline reappeared on the scene and walked to where Samuel stood. "Chastity is in your office playing video games on the computer," Pauline whispered in Samuel's ear, then noticed Woodrow approaching them. She hurriedly took her place in one of the plush chairs behind them.

"Boy, what happened in here?" Woodrow asked above a whisper with a scowl drawn on his face.

"I am about to explain everything now, Pops," Samuel impatiently said and sighed.

People were crying and it seemed like all the chaos was because of Ms. Jessie's demise. The ambulance arrived to collect her frail old frame and covered her up on the gurney. Monroe and a few of the congregants hung around crying and shaking their heads as they watched the dead woman being lifted away.

"I'm really sorry, everybody," Monroe said to them, then dropped his head and walked toward the pew while Meesha stared and continued chumping on her Doritos like she was watching a horror movie in front of her very eyes.

131

"That poor old woman," Meesha said with a mouthful of chips. "She was a sweet old woman. I'm going to miss her. Honey, may Jesus be with her," she continued as she pulled a double cheeseburger out of her purse and chewed loudly on it.

Samuel grimaced at her and frowned a little bit. This woman can eat for fifteen. As long as I've known her ass, there has never been a time when she wasn't eating. She's the size of a UPS truck, and she complains about being overweight like she doesn't know the cause. Maybe if she pushed away from the table, she wouldn't have to worry about it breaking when she presses on it to feed her fat ass face, Samuel thought.

Meesha was a 31-year-old published author, script writer, and psychology major. She weighed about 325 pounds and was five feet, eleven inches tall. Her natural hair was usually coifed in a fro-hawk and she had an obsession with the retired football player, Will Demps. Meesha was a holier-than-thou virgin who constantly complained about being fat, and she was so determined to snag a man like Will Demps.

"Sister Meesha, why don't you have a seat," Samuel said while thinking, She needs a seat for two.

"Sure, Pastor Baker," she said and took a bite out of a strawberry cupcake that had mysteriously appeared in her hand.

And she wonders why she can't get a man. I don't think Will Demps would ever give her the time of the day, because he'd end up spending most of his earnings feeding her. The best way he'd be able to make love to her would be by shoving a cheese burger down her damn throat, Samuel thought as he shook his head at her and returned to the pulpit. The camera crew wasn't present since he normally didn't televise funerals, and he was grateful for that.

"Everybody, today has been a trying day for us, but I always tell you that God has a way of talking to us in mysterious ways. The Lord puts us through trials and tribulations to test our faith in him. Ms. Jessie was another important aspect to our community but it was her time to go," Samuel said and looked back at his father who gave him a scowl that was so ugly he could have scared the Boogie Man to death. Samuel flinched a little and cleared his throat to think about what he was going to say next to the massive crowd. But before he could say anything else, one of his members intervened.

"You say God works in mysterious ways, but why would he kill an elderly woman for the heck of it? He didn't kill her. She died from what your daughter said," the aging, rail thin man stated from the crowd.

Samuel frowned in concentration as he tried make out what the guy was saying. The rest of the congregation members were giving the guy wild looks and speaking amongst one another. "I'm sorry brother, I cannot hear you from here. Would you mind coming to the front of the microphone stand to speak your piece about Sista Jessie and Rosetta?" Samuel asked.

The man was in the front row and he quickly strolled down the aisle. He approached the microphone stand and spoke into the microphone. The look on the man's ghastly face confirmed his displeasure for Samuel. "I am sick and tired of preachers like you blaming everything on God. That poor woman didn't die from God. She died because of what your daughter said. How sickening of you to blame God for that poor old woman's demise. You're a fraud and a pulpit vulture," the guy spat and pointed at Samuel.

"I beg your pardon, brother?" Samuel said with a perplexed look.

"You heard what the hell I said, you fraudulent bastard! And I am not your damn brother. You either

134

blame God or use him as a cover up for your deception and tomfoolery. You're no different from T.D. Snakes, Klepto Dolla, Benny Sinn, Jesse "KKK" Peterson, that faggot ass Eddie Long Shlong Strokes, and Rob Parsley," the angry man blustered.

"How dare you disrespect Pastor Baker and all those other honorable men, especially Eddie Long? He who is without sin, let him cast the first stone!" said a hefty, light-skinned man wearing bifocals, and suspenders to keep his pants pulled up over his rotund belly.

"Amen," said the rest of the members.

"You've probably got more skeletons than a cemetery and you think you can come inside of the Lord's house and disrespect him and one of his children? As a gay white man, I am highly offended for your race and the things you're saying about Eddie Long, during the wake of one of the most memorial figures in the black community; you're disrespecting her legacy the way her children did! You all need help!" the gay member shouted.

"Amen," shouted the rest of members. Their agreement with the two members who'd bravely challenged the angry man incited a surge of anger inside of him that sent him on another rampage.

"All of you can go to hell in a cardboard box without a rest stop! And as for you, fag boy, I wouldn't be surprised if Mr. Long Shlong stroked your boy coochie! All of you sick reprobates need to purchase my new book entitled, "Faggots, Bull Daggers, and Pimps in the Pulpit". You can purchase it through my website called, AbominationsMustDie.com, the angry man boasted.

"Why don't you plug your book up your ass," the gay member taunted and flipped the angry man off.

"I could probably plug my foot up your faggot ass but you'd probably enjoy the sensation!" The angry man shot back. And then he directed his anger toward the hefty light-skinned fellow. "And you'd better watch what you say, because word on the street is your wife's been having an affair with some porn star named, Sir-Fuck-A lot, who is known for sucking his own penis and the penis of Pastor Baker's nasty ass old daddy, Woodrow," the angry man revealed.

People started gasping and the gasps and shocking revelations were so overwhelming they could have shattered all the windows in the church.

Woodrow looked like he wanted to hide for cover, but instead he stood up and decried the angry man's accusations. "Those are wicked lies if I ain't heard any.

136

You are one disgraceful devil. I ought to beat the hell out of you!" Woodrow threatened and tried to charge at the angry man, but Samuel held him back.

"Not until I whip his ass first," the hefty light-skinned man said, but he was pulled back by the members around him."

"Lord, have mercy. I cannot take anymore of this," Pauline said and erupted into tears as she ran to join her daughter in the back.

"Doggone it, let me go," Woodrow said while struggling with Samuel to get free.

"No," Samuel said. It was the first time in his adult life that he'd challenged his father's demands.

"You're going to learn to respect your elders, boy! I'm going to beat you like I was your daddy!" Woodrow struggled to say to the man, as he unsuccessfully tried to peel his son's grip off his arms.

"Go buy yourself a respirator before you go gunning off at the mouth about kicking someone's ass, you self-righteous old pervert. And as for you, Mr. Piggy," the angry man turned and pointed at the hefty man again, "you need to lose a lot of weight and gain a lot of awareness because your whore of a wife has more DNA in her than an FBI database."

"Screw you, you lying buzzard! Baby, it isn't true what he's saying; I promise," the man's wife said in a shaky tone and tried to calm him down.

Samuel was able to calm Woodrow down and get him to sit down, then he ordered his ushers to remove the disruptive man from the church. "I want this man out of my church expeditiously!" Samuel ordered.

The ushers started in the man's direction to do as they were told, and the angry man held his hands up to surrender. "

Alright, I'm leaving, but there is one more thing I need to show you," he said while pulling something out of his coat pocket that looked like a book. "You guys can purchase my book for $12.99 and be infused with the truth and nothing but the bold and the ugly truth! If all of you don't turn your backs on these devils in the pulpit, you are doomed for hell. Especially if you're a follower of this fool over here," the angry man said as he pointed his finger at Samuel.

"And Bridgette Brice is a usurper of the devil for saying that it is okay to be gay. She's pimping all of you dumb ass black women and she's trying to turn you all out and away from all men so that you can become man-hating freaks just like her," the man rambled on.

"Alright, we've had enough out of you to last two centuries," one of the tall lanky ushers muttered as he tried to escort the angry man out of the church.

"Don't put your hands on me. Don't touch me. I will escort my damn self out. Damn all of you to hell. I promise I'll never return to this wicked den of iniquity for as long as I am speaking and spreading the truth," the guy said as he was being escorted out by the ushers.

The rest of the members called him names while the hefty light-skinned man's wife was still trying to convince her husband that she wasn't being unfaithful. Samuel was completely baffled and his expression turned stony. He wasn't completely mad at the man about his comments about pastors who fed off their congregations, and he certainly couldn't have agreed with the man more about Bridgette Brice, because he carried similar feelings about her sexuality.

However, with all of the perpetual chaos in his personal life and the fracas in his church, Samuel finally made a sound decision right that moment that he was going to announce that he'd be taking some time away from church to unclutter his mind.

"Ladies and gentlemen, with everything that has been happening lately, I've decided that I will be taking some time off from church so that I can get my mind right. I am fighting with some personal demons and I need to resolve those issues. I ask you to keep me and my family in your utmost prayers. Thank you and God bless you," Samuel revealed and stepped away from the pulpit.

The congregation began to mill around and speak amongst themselves like they'd just heard that Samuel had died instead of being told that he was going to take a temporary leave of absence from the church.

Woodrow quickly jumped out of his seat and approached Samuel with so much contempt on his face, he looked like a gargoyle. "Boy, what's with you? You can't just walk away from the church like that," he scolded above a whisper.

"Pop, I need to take some time off to clear my head. I cannot keep depriving myself of a much needed break. Besides, I don't get to spend as much time with my family as I'd like to and this would be the perfect time for that," Samuel whispered.

Woodrow's face hardened; if it had gotten any stonier, it would have cracked into pieces. He didn't say anything to Samuel, but snatched the microphone out of his hands, which took Samuel by surprise. "My son wasn't serious about what he said. He just had a moment of insanity. That's all. Tell 'em, son," Woodrow said with a nervous smile, but gave Samuel a warning look with his eyes.

The crowd settled down a little and waited for Samuel's response. Samuel took the microphone from Woodrow's hands and stared intently at the crowd. "Like I said earlier, I am taking a temporary leave of absence from the church and I will return shortly after," he stated to the members.

The members began complaining again and Woodrow tried to pry the microphone out of his hands. "Boy, have you gone mad? Don't tell me you're tucking your penis between your legs and wimping out? I raised you better than that. You need to tell these people the truth," Woodrow remarked and shook his fist. Every time his mouth jutted, the extra skin that hung from his chin jiggled.

"And that's just the problem; you raised me," Samuel mumbled and faced the crowd.

"What did you say, boy?" Woodrow asked with enough exasperation on his face to scare the beige walls white.

Samuel ignored his father's question and resumed addressing the mass. "Okay, folks, please settle down," he instructed and the congregants finally quieted down. They got so quiet, you could've heard a mouse sneeze. Woodrow was burning a hole into the back of Samuel's head with his fiery red, bloodshot eyes, but Samuel didn't care. "Now, you all know I am a man of my word and when I say I'm going to do something, I always do it. I know you guys honor me, but you must honor God first. Exodus 20:1-3 reads, 'And God spake all these words, saying, I am the LORD your God, which have brought thee out of the land of Egypt, out of the house of bondage. Thou shalt have no other gods before me.' You all should also read Deuteronomy 6:4-5, Mark 12:28-33, and John 3:11-23. I need to do some soul searching, and I am going to need for all of you to bear with me, because the Lord is. My father and another pastor will cover for me while I am away and they will preside over Sister Rosetta's funeral. I know they will also keep you updated about Ms. Jessie's funeral, too. May the Lord be with Ms. Jessie and Sister Rosetta," Samuel said with pseudo humility.

"Amen," said the congregation.

"How long are you going to be gone?" asked the young, smooth face, dark-skinned woman who sat in the front pew. Her eyes were red from all the crying she'd done, and she blotted her eyes to prevent the fresh tears from rolling down her face.

"I shouldn't be gone for any more than a couple of weeks. But while I am away, I'll be thinking about all of you and praying for you as much you're praying for me. I know this is hard on most of you, but it is necessary. Please understand that I am not doing it for myself, but I am doing it for all of you. I encourage all of you to make peace with Sista Rosetta and make the best out of the rest of your day, because she would have wanted it that way. I must leave now. Thank you and God bless you," Samuel said in closing. He placed the microphone on the stand, departed from the pulpit and walked to his office.

Woodrow's eyes grew so wide, they looked like they were going to explode. His mouth hung open so wide, if it'd gotten any wider, his jaw would have broken. After a few seconds, he closed his mouth and plastered a pseudo smile on his face. "Pardon me, ladies and gentlemen," he said and quickly retreated to the office after Samuel.

Chastity was in the office drawing and coloring on construction paper and Pauline was sitting next to her re-braiding one of her loose ponytails. When Samuel entered the office, he startled Pauline.

"Oh my God," she said as she clutched her chest and breathed heavily. "You almost scared the baby of me," she added and pursed her lips tightly.

"I'm sorry, baby. I feel like I'm losing my mind. You and I—" Samuel started.

"Boy, you've either handed your sanity check to the devil for him to cash it or you've become a one-man army against God and me. I don't know what's gotten into you, boy, but you've got two minutes before I—" Woodrow interrupted as he rushed into the office.

"Daddy Woodrow, is everything okay?" Pauline interrupted and asked with a surprised look painted on her face.

Woodrow shot her look that would have made a vampire blister. "Woman, does it look like everything is okay?! I swear you're as dumb as a jelly bean. And what have I told you about meddlin' when me and my son are conversatin'?"

"Pops, that's enough, okay?" Samuel sternly said and stood beside Pauline, who was rubbing her belly and trying hard to suppress her tears.

"Come again, boy?" Woodrow asked and cupped his hand behind his ear to make sure he'd heard Samuel correctly.

"I said, that's enough, okay?" Samuel repeated in the same stern voice. That's when Pauline's sad face turned into a half smile. She was proud of Samuel for finally standing up to his father.

"Boy, if my granddaughter wasn't sitting at this desk, I'd make you eat everything you said just now," Woodrow said with his lips curled and his fists balled.

Pauline sensed trouble brewing because her eyes grew as large as fish eyes; she gripped Samuel's hands tighter for security just in case things got ugly, but Samuel gently unfastened his hands from hers. Samuel quickly glanced at Chastity to see if she was watching the entire debacle, but thankfully, she was too engrossed in her drawing and coloring to notice a soul. So, Samuel redirected his attention back to Woodrow, who was ready to tear into him.

"Do you mind if we go outside for a minute, Pop?" he said in a more level tone.

"No. Whatever it is that's messing with your senses, you can tell me right here, straight to my face, with no chaser," Woodrow spat and kept his fists tight.

"Okay, fine. Pauline and I are going on a long overdue vacation for a few weeks," Samuel announced.

"We are?" Pauline asked while looking dumbfounded.

"Yes, we are," Samuel said without taking his eyes off his father's stare, which was cold and fiery at the same time.

"And since when did you decide to take a vacation without speaking to me first?" Woodrow asked and clenched his fists tighter. His facial expression transformed from angry to furious.

"I was going to tell you, but it kind of happened at the spur of the moment," Samuel lied and looked at Pauline with an uneasy expression.

"So,`2 you think about things without coming to me first and then you wait until that mishap out there to take place to finally bitch out like a sissy, and say that you and your little simple wife here are going on vacation? You got some sissified nerve, boy!" Woodrow unclenched and clenched his fists like he was preparing to hit Samuel.

"Pop, I'd appreciate if you refrained from insulting my wife and using that kind language in front of Chastity. She's heard more than enough to last her until she's

21. This isn't the right place to use that kind of tone or language anyway," Samuel reminded.

Woodrow's eyes narrowed into slits and his lips curled up again. "You've got until later this evening to change your mind or you and I are going to have some problems," Woodrow threatened, then shook his finger in Samuel's face and nearly touched his nose.

"I'm afraid that isn't going to happen, Pop. Also, instead of you and another pastor, I have decided I'm going to ask Pastor Lumpkin and Pastor Rankin to cover for me while Pauline and I are on vacation," Samuel calmly said.

"Pastor Lumpkin and Pastor Rankin? Now, I know you've gone mad, boy! You know how much I can't stand those doggone heathens!" Woodrow shouted and stomped like Rumpelstiltskin.

"Pop, let's go outside and talk. This isn't the kind of conversation I feel comfortable having in front of Pauline and Chastity. Pauline, I'll be back. I need to talk to Pop for a minute," Samuel stated and walked out of the office with Woodrow in tow.

"Okay, sweetheart," Pauline nervously said and went back to re-braiding Chastity's hair.

Once Samuel and Woodrow were outside, Woodrow started ranting. "Boy, if this is some kind of joke, it ain't funny, because Pastor Lumpkin doesn't even have a lot of members at his church; he's got that jumpy eye that tells me he's a snake in the green grass. And Pastor Rankin still owes me for breaking my fishing rod. I figured you'd at least have the decency to deal with Pastor Morley and Pastor Lovelace. You sure know how to pick 'em,boy," Woodrow spat, as if the names he'd mentioned tasted like spoiled milk.

"First of all, Pastor Lumpkin is a great guy; he has a jumpy eye because he has poor vision due to a childhood accident. And you told me when you went fishing with Pastor Rankin, you caught a fish that was so big it yanked the fishing rod and you had to let it go to avoid falling in the water," Samuel noted.

"Boy, don't try to make me out to be a lying crook when—"

Samuel continued his explanation and talked over Woodrow as if he hadn't even spoken. "Ninety-eight percent of Pastor Morley's church members are women and he has stripper poles in the center of his church; he pimps more whores and slams more doors than Super Fly. That man has more women's phone numbers than a Florida telephone book, and his wife,

Rudy is a madam who runs an escort service in the back of the church called, "Big Booty Rudy Bunny Ranch," Samuel pointed out.

Woodrow tried to protest, of course, but Samuel cut him off again. "Now, you know that is nothing but lies because—"

"And Pastor Lovelace has an ATM machine in his church and sends invoices to his church members for not paying their tithes on time. He even has his own personal collection agent go after members who can't pay their tithes at all. Plus, he makes some of his other members pay with EBT if they can't pay with cash, money order, debit or credit," Samuel revealed and scratched his head.

Woodrow was caught dead in his tracks, but he didn't want to admit that Samuel was right. "Don't you go sassing me, boy. You can learn a few things from those men," Woodrow said, shaking his fist.

"If my memory serves me correctly, you're rumored to be a secret loyal member of the "Big Booty Rudy Bunny Ranch" and Rudy sells sex tapes that her whores and their clients make, on porno sites. You wouldn't happen to know anything about that, would you?" Samuel sarcastically challenged.

Woodrow stepped up into Samuel's face and his hot funky breath made Samuel's long eyelashes curl, but he didn't flinch. "Don't you get smart with me, boy. You're campaigning for an ass whooping and you're about to get elected for four terms!" Woodrow threatened. He was about to attack Samuel, but Pauline came out in the nick of time.

"What on earth?" Pauline gasped and cupped her mouth again.

"It's nothing, darling. Pop and I were just having a discussion. Weren't we, Pops?" Samuel said with a derisive smirk on his face.

Woodrow didn't say anything. He pouted and breathed so hard his nostrils looked like two black furious eyes. Woodrow learned closer to Samuel and whispered something to him instead. "I'm going to put my foot so far up your ass you'll be pissing shoe polish for months," Woodrow said with his teeth clenched.

Instead of backing away, Samuel learned closer to Woodrow and whispered, "And if I were you, I wouldn't think about it or try it." Then he walked away from Woodrow, leaving him looking like a shocked fool.

"Everything is fine, sweetheart. You and I need to discuss our vacation plans. I'll talk to you later, Pop," Samuel said with the same sarcastic smirk on his face.

"This ain't over, boy. Ya hear? It ain't over!" Woodrow said in a threatening tone and shook his fist again.

"Well, it is for now. I need you to speak to the ushers and let them know what is going on. I also need you to contact Pastor Rankin and Lumpkin and bring them up to speed. Thanks Pop," Samuel said and closed the door in Woodrow's face without giving him the opportunity to say another word. Samuel felt good about finally standing up to his father for the very first time in his life, but he also sensed a war brewing between him and his father that he knew he wasn't prepared for.

Chapter 9

Oh, What A Night…

Samuel and Pauline were in the living room conversing about their ideal place to go on vacation and Chastity was up in her room playing with her dolls. Samuel was preoccupied and only gave Pauline half of his attention because he was still feeling uneasy about the whole Nadine thing; he still hadn't heard from Roy since the incident either. He knew he needed to speak to someone, and the only person with sound judgment who had a way of making things easier was Richie. Samuel decided he'd give Richie a call later that evening.

Surprisingly, Woodrow didn't show up unannounced, nor did he bother to call Samuel. Samuel couldn't have been more elated about it.

"Instead of going out on an exotic vacation, how about we visit my mother? She always asks when we're going to bring Chastity to visit," Pauline suggested.

Samuel sucked his teeth and sighed. "Pauline, you know how your mother is. She has a serious gambling problem and she had the nerve to marry that child molester, Sylvester. You already know how I feel about child molesters. I am not going to have my child in the company of one."

"He paid all of his dues to society and he's a changed church-going man now."

"I don't give a care how many years he served in prison. Anyone who inappropriately touches a child should be put to death." Samuel pulled out his Bible and turned to the book of Revelation. "Revelation 21:8 says, But the fearful, and unbelieving, and the abominable, and murderers, and whoremongers, and sorcerers, and idolaters, and all liars, shall have their part in the lake which burneth with fire and brimstone: which is the second death'," Samuel said and closed his Bible.

"And it also says that God forgives those who are willing to change, which means Sylvester will be granted a second chance if he doesn't revert back to his old ways. He isn't faithless because he believes in God and he faithfully goes to church," Pauline remarked and rolled her eyes.

"That is true, but what if he does revert back to his old ways? What if he never changed?" Samuel challenged.

"I am not going to get into all of this, because I believe he's a changed man. If God is willing to forgive people, so should you, Samuel Lee Baker," Pauline sternly said and reached for the TV Guide.

"You know what? I am done talking about this because there's just no getting through to you," Samuel said and threw his hands in the air.

"Dear, let's not fight again. It's been six months since I've seen my mother. I really miss her and I know she misses us too. If you don't want to do it for me, at least do it for our baby," Pauline whined and rubbed her growing belly.

Samuel sucked his teeth; he did that when Pauline got him to go against some of his decisions. "I'll do it this time because you're pregnant, but after the baby is born, I don't want our children around that pervert. Understood?" Samuel said with his eyebrows raised.

"But what about my mother? She's going to want to see the baby," Pauline wailed.

"Then she'll just have to come and visit us to see the baby. I'll pay for her plane ticket, but that's where it stops," Samuel reasoned.

"Okay, but under one condition though," Pauline said.

"What's that?"

"You must go with me to see Bridgette Brice for marriage counseling."

"Not that again. We've already discussed it. I'm not going through with it."

"Listen; you don't want Sylvester around the kids and I reluctantly agreed. Well, the least you can do is attend a couple of counseling sessions to repair our marriage. You cannot have your cake and eat it too," Pauline complained.

Samuel sighed again and agreed with her. "Fine, but only if you agree to one other condition."

"Which is?"

"I do not want Chastity coming along to your mother's, because I don't want her around that character. I'll pay Etta Rose extra money to babysit her while we're away."

Pauline nodded her head. "I am fine with those terms," she said and resumed sifting through the TV Guide.

Samuel sat on the couch next to her and touched her knee. She touched his hand with her free hand and smiled at him. "I'll try my best to behave when I am around him, but I am not letting him off the hook," he said and grabbed the remote to turn on the TV.

"I understand, baby. But once you open up to Sylvester, he's a real sweetheart," Pauline said while perusing the TV Guide.

"Does he have kids?" Samuel inquired and began flipping through the channels.

"Yes, he does, and he has grandkids," said Pauline.

Samuel put down the remote and looked at her with stern eyes. "Does he see his grandkids?"

"Well, he and his daughter aren't close," Pauline said nervously. She began to fidget with the TV Guide and avoided eye contact.

"And why is that?" Samuel asked as his face slowly morphed into a scowl. Pauline didn't say anything. "Pauline?"

"Yes?" she quietly said without looking at him.

"Why aren't he and his daughter close?" Samuel impatiently asked. Pauline bit her bottom lip, then closed her lips tightly together and opened her mouth to speak; before she could utter the next sentence, Samuel added, "And do not lie for him. Remember what the Bible says about lying. Proverbs 6:19, Leviticus 19:12, and Exodus 23:1."

"I...wasn't... going to...lie... for... him," she slowly said and exhaled a little.

"Then come out and say it," Samuel huffily said.

"Sylvester's daughter doesn't talk to him because he molested her from the time she was four years old until she was twelve," Pauline blurted and exhaled heavily.

"That does it. We're not going," Samuel said and resumed flipping the channels.

"Listen, we've both agreed that we wouldn't bring Chastity around, and you're supposed to be a man of your word," Pauline complained and pouted.

"He should be incarcerated for committing such a sick sadistic sin! You know that God doesn't condone that kind of behavior, and I for certain don't."

"You're right. It's sickening, but obviously God has forgiven him, and so should you. His daughter will forgive him too—someday. You need to give him the benefit of the doubt and remember that saints didn't always sing, like when Papa Woodrow braces the scene! Let he who is without sin cast the first stone. We must never judge nor hold grudges, no matter what the matter may be."

"Fine, whatever, but I have nothing to say to that bastard. I'm only doing this for you. My feelings and thoughts will never change about him, and I must say that his daughter has the right to feel the way she does. Are we clear on that?"

"That's fine with me. His daughter will have to have the forgiveness conversation with God alone and find peace within herself. Just promise you won't say anything to upset Mother."

"I can't promise you anything, but I'll try my best not to beat the hell out of him. The Bible clearly speaks against incest; Leviticus 18:6 says, 'None of you shall approach to any that is near of kin to him, to uncover their nakedness: I am the LORD'."

"But he's a changed man, Samuel. I assure you that he will grow on you if you give him a chance."

"He'll only grow on me like fungus," Samuel angrily quipped.

"Be nice, dear. I am going to phone Mother and let her know we're coming to visit her. By the way, when are we going?" Pauline questioned, while reaching for the phone under the lamp.

"We'll see her this week, on Thursday. I'll book a flight for the both of us, and be sure to contact Etta Rose. We're going to need her to sit in for us and babysit Chastity while we're away," he reminded.

"Okay, great. No problem." Pauline was excited and she began dialing her mother's number.

The doorbell rang and Samuel wondered who could be at his door that time of evening. He approached the door and nearly collapsed when he saw Roy through the peephole. He opened the door and quickly stepped outside. Roy was wearing all black, had a pair of shades on, and his cornrows looked like they'd been freshly braided.

"What the hell are you doing here?" Samuel asked in a stage whisper and looked around to see who may have been watching.

"I just came by to holla at you for a little minute. I apologize about what happened, but you know I had to take care of that shit for you, man. How's everything?" Roy nonchalantly said, pulled out a blunt and lit it up.

"Man, have you lost your damn mind? And don't smoke that mess on my porch!" Samuel scolded and continued looking over his shoulders to check for any nosy neighbors or his wife.

"Alright, dawg, calm down. My bad," Roy laughed and extinguished the blunt.

Samuel cut straight to the chase. "Man, I can't associate myself with you because I have too much to lose, and I don't want my name being caught up in some kind of murder rap. I need you to le—"

"Calm down, dawg. I'm good friends with a cop and he knows all about the case," Roy interrupted.

"What the hell? He knows you murdered Nadine?" Samuel questioned and nearly passed out on the porch, but he grabbed a seat to prevent himself from falling.

"I want you to sit down and let me explain everything to you."

"That's what I'm doing. This better be good," Samuel said in a threatening tone and sat in one of the guest chairs.

"Okay, the cop that I know said he knew that bitch because she was one of his mistresses. His name is Luke Pennington."

"Really? Wow…" Samuel was stunned.

"Yep, and he said he used to pay her to drop dope and weed off for him, and some of the product would always come up short. He found out she was stealing the drugs and the money, so he confronted her about it. She denied she had anything to do with it. Luke and I've known each other for years; when he and I spoke over the phone, and I told him about the bitch, it was like a symphony in his ears," Roy said and pulled out a cigarette. He lit it and took a long pull on it.

"But what about the investigation? Aren't the police going to question witnesses?" Samuel inquired.

"Yeah, they'll do their routine investigation, but I paid Luke off. So, once the investigation is over, it will be a closed case," Roy nonchalantly said and continued smoking.

"You shouldn't have killed her. I'd like for you to repent and pray with me," Samuel offered.

Roy gave him a smug look, stubbed his cigarette out on the ground and laughed. "People like me ain't gonna make it to heaven, dawg. I'm too far gone. I've murdered, stolen, robbed, racketeered, lied, and bribed people. God washed his hands of me a long time ago. I figured, why try to make it right with him, when I know there is someone who is ready to kill my black ass if I slip up one good time. Naw, this is all that I know. I don't know how to be legit like you."

"That isn't true, Roy. You're a smart man. All you need is for someone to give you a second chance. And I know God will give you one if you give your life to him. All you have to do is talk to him."

"Man, I don't know how to pray and shit. I ain't one for getting all emotional and shit, but I gotta tell you something. And when I tell you, I want you to take this shit to your grave, alright?" Roy said with a look that was so serious, the plants on the front porch flinched.

His change in attitude kind of caught Samuel off guard, because out of all the years he'd known Roy, he'd never known him to exhibit his vulnerability to anyone. "Sure, man. I promise not to tell a breathing soul. Go ahead and sit down and talk to me," Samuel said.

Roy slightly dropped his head and shook it. "Naw, dawg. I'm good. I'll stand up," he said with uneasiness in his voice and demeanor. He dipped his hands in his pockets and he looked pensively at the sky. He didn't say anything for a few minutes, and Samuel waited patiently for him to gather his thoughts and say something. "I love you like a brother, but I also envy you," Roy commented.

Samuel's eyes grew as large as shiny saucers and his mouth hung open a little. "Why do you envy me?"

Roy looked at Samuel but he didn't say anything for about another minute. Then he divulged what was on his mind. "I envy you because you're a greater man than me. I mean, I've watched you grow from an uncertain young man to a full-fledged rich family man. I am not one to say this to another man, but I wish I could trade places with you, man." Roy dug his hands deep into his pockets.

Samuel was caught off guard by Roy's statement. All he could do was sit in the chair and stew in his shocked thoughts.

"Listen, man; I know that is something you ain't used to hearing from me and all, but you know I ain't used to confessing my feelings about shit," Roy hesitatingly said and shifted his weight to avoid eye contact with Samuel.

"It's okay, man. But I do hope you plan to make it right with God, because this is ugly and I can barely look myself in the face after what you did. I have no idea why you want to be like me because I am no more proud of the man I am, than you are of yourself." Samuel scratched his head and buried it between his hands.

The tension between them was so thick it could have choked all the gnats that were floating around them. "You know I'd lay my life down for you, dawg. You're like the big little brother I never had. And before I let anyone come along to fuck up what you've built, I'll off them like a light switch," Roy said with conviction and swatted at one of the gnats floating in the air.

Samuel straightened his posture and gave Roy a stern look. He was ready to disassociate himself from Roy so that he could iron out his ruffled thoughts and life, but he still wanted to give Roy the benefit of the doubt. He was also praying that Roy would turn his life around and unsubscribe to his insidious lifestyle.

"You don't want to be like me, Roy. In fact, you want to be better than me and yourself. But you're going to have to get baptized and become a renewed person in the name of Jesus."

Roy waved Samuel off like he was one of those annoying gnats. "Naw, man. Like I said, I am too far gone. I haven't prayed since I lost my mama. When she died, a part of me died with her."

Samuel was now intrigued, because Roy had never spoken about his family. All Samuel knew about Roy were the perpetual criminal activities he was involved in. Roy wasn't sentimental about family, and as far as Samuel knew, he was the only family Roy had. Perhaps that was why Roy had acquired the lifestyle he had. "You know, in all the years we've known one another, you've never spoken about your family. I am really sorry about your mother, man. How old were you when she died and were you two close?" Samuel inquired with a gaze.

"Well…" Roy said while wracking his brain for the first sentence he could find.

Samuel waited patiently again, folded his leg across his thigh and clasped his fingers together.

Roy sighed and recounted the fond memories he and his mother had shared. "She died on my eighth birthday. She and I were tighter than a hood rat's braids. My mama was the most beautiful woman on the earth; she looked like Dorothy Dandridge and Lena Horne rolled into one. She had countless boyfriends, but they all treated her like shit. My dad cheated on her with an 18-year-old Italian girl. So, it was only the two of us afterwards."

"So, were your parents married?" Samuel asked.

"My parents never married. They met in a club and then she got pregnant with me. My mama loved my father very much. She put up with all of his bullshit and infidelity; even when he got that Italian girl pregnant while they were together, and brought his lover and baby around me and her—son of a bitch."

Samuel gasped. "Wow, man. That is something else," he replied.

"Man, that is half the size of it," Roy commented and lit up another cigarette.

"Well, what's the other half?" Samuel asked.

Roy exhaled a waft of smoke through his nose and mouth and resumed telling the story. "My father always wanted to have his cake and eat it too. He told my mother that if he couldn't have her, no one else could. My father was a numbers runner and a rolling stone. My mother would bail him out of jail whenever he got caught up in bullshit on the streets, and she took all of his ass whippings like a champ. But when she told him she no longer wanted to be with him one day, he knocked her unconscious and doped her up with battery acid. I felt completely helpless and I feel responsible till this day." Roy's voice cracked a little and he pulled hard on his cigarette before he continued.

Samuel was speechless and stared at Roy in disbelief.

"I vowed when I found the muthafucka I was going to kill him and—"

"So…did you do it?" Samuel interrupted with one eyebrow lifted higher than the other.

"Let's just say his body parts are scattered all over the earth," Roy said in an eerie tone and he extinguished his cigarette on the ground.

Samuel couldn't find his voice or thoughts because his mind went blank and his voice disappeared. He couldn't move.

"So, answer this question for me, Mr. Pastor. How the fuck could God allow some shit like that to happen to my mama, huh?! She didn't deserve that bullshit, and when she died I stopped believing in him. He watched that bastard kill my mother and he ain't do shit about it except let him walk around free in the streets. So, I waited until I got older and I took matters into my own goddamn hands, ya dig?" Roy rubbed his eyes and sniffled a little.

"Listen, Roy. I am really sorry about your mother. I really am, man. Your mother isn't dead though, because she's in heaven. And do you think she would want you committing all these heinous crimes? Killing and robbing aren't going to bring her back," Samuel replied in a soothing voice.

"Save that bullshit sermon for the congregation, okay?" Roy scathingly said.

"Fine, I'll do that, but just remember one thing," Samuel stood and continued, "I don't want you around me or my family until you change your tune. And I don't want to hear about my name being attached to a murder."

"I got that taken care of. I assure you that your name will remain clear. As far as me changing my tune, I don't think I can ever turn back. But I do understand that you have a reputation to protect and I will always love you like a brother."

"Thanks. One more thing," Samuel said.

"Wussup," Roy replied.

"Aside from everything we've discussed, I want to forget that we've had the discussion about murder. And if you ever decide to turn your life around, please do not be a stranger."

"Alright, bruh. That definitely sounds like a plan. Much respect and blessings to you," Roy said with a smile and gave Samuel a pound.

Samuel returned the pound, minus the smile. He was really hoping that Roy would keep his word.

~~   ~~

"Hey brotha man. What's up," Richie answered on the second ring. Samuel sighed and wiped the perspiration off his forehead; his conscience was relentlessly harassing him.

"I'm not well, man. That is why Pauline and I are going on a vacation," Samuel said.

"Oh, where to?"

"Well, Pauline and I are going out of town to see her parents but I am not too keen about seeing her despicable stepfather. And for the most part, my spirit is troubled."

"Why don't you want to see her stepfather? What's the matter? And what about the funeral?" Richie was shooting off questions like an AK-47.

"One of the pastors I know will be presiding over Sista Rosetta's funeral. My wife's stepfather's name is Sylvester and he's a child molester. He molested his own daughter when she was a child and now she doesn't speak to him. My wife claims he's a church-going God-fearing man now and she wants me to forgive him."

"Oh, okay. Wow, brotha man. That is crazy. So, why are you going to see him when you feel that way about him?" Richie asked.

"Oh, believe me; I don't want to see the bastard. But I had to promise my wife that we would go see her mother now if I didn't want Chastity and the baby on the way to be around him later. I also have to go with her to see Bridgette Brice."

"Bridgette Brice? As in, the lesbian Bridgette Brice?" Roy asked with surprise dripping from his voice.

"Yep, that's her. My wife said we're having problems in our marriage and we should see her. I know our marriage has been rocky at times, but I am not one to see a marriage counselor. Let alone, a gay one. This woman seduces other women into buying her books so that they can leave their husbands and become lesbians too. Hell no, I refuse to go out like that."

"I hear ya, brotha man," Roy said and laughed. "I don't mind women having their own minds, but they let this whole independence thing go straight to their heads. That is why so many of them can't get a man, especially most of these so-called black women. They walk around with stank attitudes and they flip their glued in hair weaves, thinking they're Goddess Almighty. And when they listen to devils like Bridgette Brice, who is an alleged black woman, they go stark raving mad. So, yeah, I understand where you're comin' from. It's people like her who are tryin' to emasculate men, and she must be rebuked."

"Amen to that, bro," Samuel agreed.

"I don't blame you for not wanting to be around that child molester either. You have to be—pardon my Portuguese—a sick piece of shit to sexually abuse a child. I don't blame you for not wanting to be in the same room with him. I hope I'm not being too harsh with ya, brotha man."

"No, speak your mind, man," Samuel praised and laughed. "I have a lot on my mind that's been troubling me and I will continue to ask Jesus for his mercy. I just needed someone to talk to and I know you're one who can make sense out of things. I really appreciate it, man."

"It's not a problem, brotha man. But it's funny you called me because I was telling my homeboy, Johan about you. He's a Hebrew Israelite, and I must say he is a very deep brother. He's showing me so many things I never learned in church, and for some reason, I thought of you, because you're not the average pastor."

"What do you mean by that?" Samuel incredulously asked while furrowing his eyebrows.

"No, it isn't what you think, man," Roy laughed again. "It's in a good way. You're not the average pastor. You are not afraid to show your sensitive side and you don't hold back the things that trouble you when you speak to me. Most pastors are stiff like ironing boards and they forget that they're still human beings. And not only that, you're down to earth and you're real."

"Wow, thanks, man. That is very kind of you. But I do feel that I need to be more honest with myself. I feel like I am trapped in a maze of my mind and I don't know how to find my way out," Samuel admitted.

"Brother man, all you have to do is give the Most High your burdens and he will deliver you. But I'd really like to introduce you to Johan. He's very deep and he drops knowledge like bombs. You'll be amazed by what you learn, brotha man," Richie said with a smile in his voice.

"And you said he's a Hebrew Israelite? Is he Jewish or something?" Samuel inquired.

That's when Richie began chuckling. "No, brotha man. He isn't Jewish. He is a proud black man who knows who he is. Besides, the Jewish people aren't even the original people or Jews."

"I beg your pardon?" Samuel said.

"You heard me, brotha man. The very Bible you teach and preach from reveals who the original Jews are. You just overlook it like all the other pastors do, but you can't help it though. You've been brainwashed and indoctrinated to believe that your savior is some white man with blue eyes and long blonde hair."

"Well, I don't know where you're getting your sources from, but the God I serve isn't white. He is the image and we are the likeness of him."

"I see. So, why is it that you have images of a feminine looking white man all over your church then? There was dead silence on the phone. Richie had struck a chord with Samuel so hard, Samuel thought he had paralysis. "Are you still there, brother man?" Richie asked.

"Yeah, um, I, um…listen, that is tradition," Samuel stuttered. "That is tradition and we all know that the Savior does not have a color. What you see is his image. It does not mean that he was white."

"Then if he wasn't white, why does he look like a pale faggot? You've yet to answer my question," Richie sardonically said.

"Jesus Christ, man. What is the matter with you? You are blaspheming the Lord's name, and it is very unbecoming of you. I don't know what that Israelite friend of yours is telling you, but he isn't a man of God. He sounds more like a cultist and he's turning you into him. You know that kind of mentality will get you excommunicated from my church like it did Terri Salters."

Richie started chuckling again and his chuckle transformed into a sinister laugh. "You know what? Brother Johan said you would say somethin' like that. And sista Terri was an atheist; she was smart enough to unlearn that crap that you be teachin' and preachin'. I love you like a brotha too, and that is why I'm speakin' to you like this, because I see the potential in you. Man, you could be the next Malcolm X for the Israelites."

Samuel started grinding his teeth in anger; he hadn't grinded his teeth in years. In fact, he didn't even do it when Nadine angered him. He had to ask himself if he was grinding his teeth because he was mad at how well Richie really knew him, but he wasn't going to tell Richie, of course.

"Richie, listen. Terri was a pot smoking, big haired, tattooed reprobate. And I feel very sorry for her little son because she is grooming him to become another infidel like her. You know the lord frowns down on sinners."

"Sure he does, but he also frowns down on blood-sucking pastors too," Richie sarcastically reminded.

"Wait, hold on a minute. Come on, Rich—" Samuel stammered and struggled to spew out his next set of words.

"Naw, brotha man. You can't throw stones from a glass house," Richie interrupted. "Terri may have been a ganja smokin' sista, but at least she ain't afraid to be honest with herself. Yeah, she was far from perfect, but she never held her tongue about anything. You may want to reevaluate yourself too."

Samuel knew Richie was right and he was grateful to have Richie in his life. "Yeah, you're right. I really do need to reevaluate myself. I've had a lot going on lately and I feel like everything is closing in on me; it's sucking the life out of me. I don't know what I'd do if I didn't have you as a friend. Thanks, man."

"That's what friends are for. But listen...I'd really love for you to meet with Johan. He can be a beacon of light in your darkness."

"I don't know about that. I mean, he sounds like one of those revolutionary Black Panther nuts."

Richie laughed out loud and shook his head. "He ain't that kind of guy. See, there you go rippin' people a new anus without givin' 'em a chance. Can you at least test the brother out first? If he still doesn't enlighten you, you can move on. Is that cool?"

Samuel sucked in his breath and cleared his throat. "Yeah, I guess it wouldn't hurt. And to be honest, I haven't been feeling very Christian-like lately, anyway," Samuel admitted.

"Oh, really? Do tell," Richie inquired with a chuckle.

"Well, I want you to keep what I'm about to share between the two of us, okay?"

"Sure, I won't tell a single soul."

"Okay, here it goes. The creepiest thing happened to me. I saw a reflection of myself in the mirror and I had dreadlocks and a long scraggly beard. The reflection spoke to me and said he was my future self; then he told me to read deeper into the King James Version of the Bible so that I can discover who I truly am. Man, I was so spooked, I felt like my nerves had goose bumps. And it happened to me twice," Samuel said and chucked his index finger and middle up to make the peace sign.

"Wow, brotha man. That is deep. See, I told you that you're one of a kind. The Most High is speaking to you. This isn't a coincidence. Dude, you're the chosen one and you don't even realize it. Speaking of the devil, that's Johan calling me right now. I'mma hit you up later, brotha man."

"Alright, cool. But do not tell him. I want to tell him myself. And we'll link up when I return from this dreadful trip with Pauline. I should be back in about a week or so," Samuel said with a sigh.

"Alright, brotha man. Try to make the best of it. At least it will give you some time to get your head together. But hey, I gotta go. Talk to you later," Richie said and the line went dead.

Samuel held the phone up to his face and sighed again before he clicked the end button. He tapped his fingers on his custom made oak wood desk. Then suddenly his mind trailed off, his eyes fluttered a little, and memories of his troubled childhood seeped in as he dozed off.

Let me tell you something, you son of a Jezebel. If I catch you listening to that devil's music again, I'm going to beat the living devil out of you!

But, Pops, this is the New Edition album. All of the kids have it.

New what?

New Ed—

Shut up, boy! I don't give a damn what they're called. You're spending my hard earned money on this garbage. Before you know it, you'll be entering my humble abode thinking you all grown and stuff and smoking that devil grass. Well, it will be over YOUR dead body!

But, Pops—

But, Pops nothing! Give me this devil record. I'm throwing it in the trash before it defiles you.

But I paid good money for this record.

No, you paid MY good money for this trash.

Give it back!

Boy, who you think you sassin'? You're campaigning to get several switch licks, and you're about to get elected for two terms!

I don't care! I want my record back. It's mine!

Not as long as I'm the head shift in this house, it ain't!

CRAAAACK!

I hate you!

WHAP!

Samuel suddenly woke up. That day was the most humiliating event in Samuel's life. When he'd told his father he hated him for confiscating his New Edition album, his father had punched him in his eye. Samuel had been unable to return to school until the bruise from the black eye vanished. While he was home healing, he'd had to write, "I will never talk back to my father again" 300 times on paper, he had to rake the leaves, wash the car, and study the Scriptures. Samuel had wanted to hate his father, but he was afraid to. He'd just wanted his father to go away and never return to his life. But since Samuel had been instilled with fear, and was commanded to love the Scriptures with all of his heart, he was afraid to think the wrong way; he was scared to go to sleep for a few nights because of it. However, he wouldn't have been able to sleep even if he'd wanted to because he could hear his father and another one of his female congregation members making love out loud in the other bedroom. It was devastating for Samuel, but standing up to his father for the first time brought about a renewal of his manhood and he had no shame. He'd smiled for the first time that night.

His mind reverted back to the conversations he'd had with Richie and Roy. Samuel was sure that he would have to let Roy go because he was detrimental to his career and freedom. And Samuel was hoping that Roy would make the right decision and turn himself into the authorities without mentioning him. If he got off, Samuel prayed that Roy would turn his life around before coming back into his life. Richie on the other hand, was real and his friendship was what Samuel needed, because he knew Richie would never steer him in a lot of bad directions the way his so-called friend Roy had. Samuel just knew when the time came, he would have to make a decision to sever all ties with Roy to save face from any controversy. Samuel felt like an air balloon because everything that he was holding in was about to make him pop. Then he thought about his future reflection in the mirror and Pauline's stepfather, who he hated more than anything in the world. Lo and behold, Pauline graced his office with her presence at the very moment those thoughts crossed his mind.

"Dear, am I interrupting anything?" Pauline asked as she lightly tapped on the door with her fingernails.

"Um, no. I just got off the phone with Pastor Lumpkin. Come in," Samuel lied and straightened his posture.

"Oh okay. How are he and Millie doing?"

"Um, they're doing great," Samuel hesitantly said.

"That's good. Will Pastor Lumpkin be covering for you?"

"Well, I'm trying to get him and Pastor Rankin to cover for me," Samuel replied with a faux cough and averted his eyes away from Pauline's.

"Honey, are you okay?" Pauline asked in a concerned tone.

"Yes, I'm fine. It's the dust, that's all," Samuel said and smiled.

"Okay, so anyway, I have great news. I called Mother and told her we'll be visiting her and Sylvester this week. Oh, and she told me that Sylvester has a surprise for us when we arrive," Pauline cheerily said.

"A surprise?" Samuel questioned with one of his eyebrows arched so high, it looked like a tall, hairy hill.

"Yes, I can't wait to know what it is." Pauline beamed and clasped her hands together with joy.

Samuel wasn't impressed by anything Sylvester did. If Sylvester rescued five old ladies from a burning building, Samuel knew he still wouldn't cut him any slack. "I'm sure whatever it is, it is probably nothing shy of a surprise," Samuel dryly said and begin scribbling something on his notepad.

Pauline sucked her teeth and folded her arms. "Samuel, when are you going to give the man a break? I mean, you speak about the dangers of holding grudges in your sermons, all the time. Those sermons should apply to you too. And I hope you don't embarrass me when we visit Mother. You already know how you get when you're in your stubborn moods." Pauline shook her head, sat down, and crossed her legs.

"That's different. He's a child molester and he may molest another child. Do you remember that televangelist T.P. Rogers? He molested his own son. That sounds close to home, because Sylvester molested his own daughter. I just hope Sylvester isn't following in T.P's footsteps— sicko!" Samuel disgustedly said.

"I understand how you feel, Samuel, but I don't think Sylvester wants to become a televangelist because Mother would have told me about it."

"And how could you be so sure?"

"Because as much as Sylvester loves the Lord, he wouldn't keep his desires to become a televangelist a secret."

Samuel sighed and gave Pauline a disgusted look. "Pauline, you put too many undesirables on the pedestal. I am beginning to think I'm married to another woman." Samuel rolled his eyes in disgust.

"No, I just give people the benefit of the doubt and I don't play God. You're a man of the cloth who plays God and you judge people without praying for them," Pauline noted.

"I am not going to continue going back and forth with you, Pauline. Besides, you are pregnant and the last thing I want to do is stress you. We will discuss this at a later time. However, I still stand strongly behind everything I said about your stepfather."

Pauline slowly rose from her seat. "Okay, fine. Are you still going to attend marriage counseling with me? I already contacted Bridgette after I got off the phone with Mother and her assistant penciled us in for the second day after we come back from visiting my folks."

Samuel gave Pauline a stare that was so wicked, she flinched and nearly choked on her breath. "I wish you would have asked me if I had any other engagements before you made that decision for the both of us. Sure, that's fine," Samuel angrily replied.

Pauline carefully chose her words out of fear of setting off Samuel's anger. "I know…but this is the best time

Bridgette…has available to see us. I would have scheduled to see her later, but we would've had to wait weeks or months to see her. But then again…we're a well-known couple and I know she wouldn't put us off like that," Pauline said with a nervous laugh as embarrassment covered her face.

"I understand that, but you should have come to me first. But what's done is done. If something comes up before then, I'll just postpone it." Pauline carefully sat back in her chair and stared intently at Samuel. Samuel gave her a suspicious look. "What's the problem? I agreed to do this marriage counseling thing with you."

"It's more than that, dear. I may not always agree with everything you say and do, and I don't always want to do the things you want to do either." Pauline shrugged her shoulders and sadness nestled in her eyes as her voice trailed off.

"What do you mean you don't always want to do the things I want to do," Samuel replied with renewed frustration.

"I think it'd be better if we saves this for the counseling session. Like you said, it isn't healthy for me to be stressed out while I'm pregnant." Pauline nervously pulled herself up from her chair like she was carrying quadruplets instead of one baby.

"Fine, Pauline. Since we agree not to discuss all of our marital problems until we speak with a lesbo marriage counselor, because we don't want to complicate your pregnancy, we will not continue this discourse until the day of the counseling session. How does that sound?" Samuel asked in a sarcastic tone.

Pauline shot him a look that was so evil, it could have killed a scorpion. She stormed out of the room and slammed the door, causing the pictures on the wall to rattle. Samuel's smirk altered into a ghastly frown and he pulled out his Chinese stress balls.

Chapter 10

Sylvester, the Child Molester...

The flight to Virginia was long and dreadful. Pauline and Samuel didn't say anything to one another throughout the entire trip. Samuel spent the duration of the trip reading his Bible and replaying all of the events that were harassing his mind and Pauline listened to music and slept most of the time. When they finally arrived at his mother-in-law's white and tan bungalow, they instantly pretended like they were the happiest couple in the world. As the cab driver helped them unload their things from the car, an older woman who looked like she could have been Pauline's older sister trotted down the stairs to greet them.

Pauline's mother, Tawny, looked identical to Pauline; she was aging gracefully. She had those same piercing yellow-brown eyes as Pauline and she was about the same size and height as her daughter. The difference was Tawny had a few tendrils of gray hair gleaming from the edges of her hairline, and she kept her hair tightly drawn into a bun. Otherwise, she was a sight for blind eyes.

Samuel paid the taxi driver and thanked him as he stood to the side and watched his mother-in-law approach.

"Good morning, darling. I've missed you so such. I'm so glad you made it here to see me and your daddy," Tawny sang as she kissed Pauline on the cheeks and hugged her.

"I missed you too, Mother." Pauline and Tawny shared an eternal embrace that could have broken the Guinness World Record for longest hug. Tawny and Pauline finally pulled away from each other to examine one another. "You look stunning as always, Mother," Pauline said with tears in her eyes.

"Oh, darling…having good genes, with a little help from daily consumption of a wheat grass shake always does the trick. But enough about me; look at you. My, my, my, child; you are glowing. I tell ya, pregnancy looks good on you. How far along did you say you are, darling?" Tawny asked with admiration.

"I'm about two months pregnant. I'm due for another check-up soon."

"Well, I sure hope it's another girl because I'd like to show her how to sew, cook, and hold on to her man," Tawny chuckled.

"Samuel and I are just hoping for a healthy baby, no matter the gender. Isn't that right, baby?" Pauline feigned a smile.

Samuel caught onto her fake smile and put on his best theatrical smile. "Absolutely, dear," he stated and smiled wider than a Cheshire Cat in a Meow Mix commercial.

"Amen to that. Anywho, speaking of babies, how's my little baby doll Chastity doing? I wish you could have brought her."

"She's doing fine. I wish I could have brought her too, but we didn't want to take her out of school so soon; Etta Rose is watching her while we're away."

"That is understandable, but you be sure that you bring her here on Thanksgiving and Christmas, because I am not having it any other way. Oh, and tell Etta Rose I said hello, and ask her if I can borrow her recipe for that mouthwatering cinnamon pumpkin pecan pie she made last Thanksgiving. Honey, that pie was so delicious it almost made me want to punch my pretty self in the face."

"Oh, Mother, you're too much," Pauline replied with an uncomfortable laugh and gave Samuel a brief glance.

Samuel kept the act going and laughed along.

"Where are my manners? It is so good to see you too, son-in-law. How are you?" Tawny gave Samuel a firm hug, but it didn't last as long as the hug she'd shared with her daughter.

"I'm fine, Ms. Tawny, and I must say, you look radiant."

"Thank you, darling, and stop calling me Ms. Tawny. You've been married to my daughter for eight years now. You can call me Mom." Tawny gave Samuel a light slap on his forearm and reached up and kissed him.

"Okay…Mom," Samuel hesitantly said and released an uncomfortable laugh.

"See, that wasn't so hard, was it?" Tawny said with a wide smile.

"Is Sylvester home?" Pauline inquired.

"No, he went out to do some mission work for the church. He shouldn't be very long though."

"But he knows we're here, right?" Pauline asked.

"Of course he does. He just needed to take care of some duties for the church first thing this morning."

"I know, but I thought he'd be here to greet us when we arrived."

"Oh, darling, you know how your father is. It's his calling and it's a daily routine for him. It's no biggie. He'll be home soon." Tawny smiled with a dismissive wave.

"Now let me help you with those bags. You shouldn't be carrying heavy things in your condition, darling."

"No, it's okay, Mom. I'll carry the bags. You and Pauline go on inside and rest your pretty arms and get caught up on lost times," Samuel said and began collecting the luggage at once.

"Why, that's mighty fine of you, Samuel," Tawny said while batting her eyelashes like a southern debutante. "You are a true gentleman. I am so blessed to have you as my son-in-law. You don't know how much I brag about you to my co-workers; I am the envy of the women at my job. Anyway, let's go inside so we can chitchat." Pauline and Tawny went inside of the house.

"I get the feeling this is going to be a very short trip," Samuel mumbled to himself and followed them into the house with the luggage.

~~ ~~

"So have you and Samuel decided what you're going to name the baby?" Tawny asked while placing the tray of iced tea on the coffee table.

Pauline leaned over to pick up a glass of iced tea. "Um, no, we're still trying to come up with a name for the child," Pauline said with an uncomfortable look on her face as she took a sip of her tea.

Tawny gave her a surprised look and placed her left hand on her hip. "You mean you and Samuel are still trying to figure out a name for your unborn child?"

"Mother, I'm still early in the pregnancy and we've been busy with the—"

"Hey, is everything alright?" Samuel interrupted as he reappeared in the living room. He'd been upstairs to drop their luggage off.

"Yes, everything is fine, dear. Mother was just asking me what we're going to name our baby," Pauline nervously said.

"Oh, yeah, we're still working on that," Samuel responded and joined the women in the room.

"Here ya go, Samuel. You look like you got your morning exercise in for the morning," Tawny chuckled and handed him the glass of tea.

"Thanks, Ms—" Samuel stopped and corrected himself. "I mean, Mom. Thanks for the tea," he laughed.

"You're welcome, darling." Tawny laughed and gave him a light tap on the shoulder.

"But we will be picking a name out for the baby soon though," Samuel stated and started gulping down his drink.

"That's right, and we're going to pick out the most beautiful name for the baby. In fact, I thought about naming the baby Samuel Baker Jr, if it's a boy," Pauline said with a beaming smile that was bright enough to light up a black city.

"Wow, I am honored, but thanks for not telling me until now," Samuel said with surprise.

"It was supposed to be a surprise," Pauline said with a smile.

"I know, baby. I'm just honored, that's all." Samuel wrapped his arms around Pauline's shoulders and kissed her soft cheek. Pauline softly rubbed his knee. It was the first time they'd conversed without arguing with each other in a while.

Tawny pensively stared at them, crossed her legs and held her tea without taking her eyes off them. "Samuel's a nice name and all, but I had a name in store for the child. No offense to you, Samuel. It's just that—oh, never mind," Tawny said with a wave of her hand and began drinking her tea.

"No, go ahead, Mother. I'm sure it's a beautiful name," Pauline encouraged.

"No, it's okay," Tawny said and resumed drinking her tea.

"Yeah, I'd like to know too," Samuel said in a slightly commanding tone.

Tawny placed her glass of tea on the table. "I thought if it's a girl, we could name her after your grandmother, Lillian; and if it's a boy, we'd name him Sylvester."

Everything went into slow motion for Samuel as he choked on his tea and coughed. Pauline patted and rubbed him on the back.

"Oh, my Lord. Are you alright, darling?" Tawny got up and rubbed his back.

"I'm fine. I'm fine, ladies," Samuel said as he gasped for air.

"Here, take this." Tawny handed him a napkin from the table. "I didn't mean to upset you."

"No, it's okay. The tea went down the wrong pipe, that's all," Samuel lied and wiped his mouth.

Tawny sighed and returned to her seat.

"Are you sure you're okay, Samuel," Pauline asked for reassurance.

"Yes, baby. I'm fine."

"I knew I shouldn't have said anything about naming the baby after Sylvester. It's my fault," Tawny said in a despondent tone.

"No it isn't, Mother. I know you meant well. But I must say that I refuse to name the baby after Grandma Lillian," Pauline uttered in a defiant tone.

Tawny shot up from her seat and her eyes nearly bubbled out of their sockets. "What do you mean you refuse to name the baby after your grandmother? I know she wasn't the sharpest tool in the tool box, but she made me promise her that I'd name her great-granddaughter after her. You know I cannot break that promise."

"Mother, I understand that, but you didn't even ask me how I felt about it. And you know how much I didn't like Grandma Lillian. She was a French bigot. That woman told me I was cursed because I was too dark to be light skinned and that my father should have married a white woman instead."

"Darling, you know your grandmother didn't mean all of those things. She was only mad at your father for marrying me at such a young age. We were both young and in love and I became pregnant with you before your father went away to Vietnam."

"Then how come she would beat me with extension cords because she said I was too dark? Mother, when you let her babysit me, that woman would force me to bathe in bleach so much that my skin would blister! Do you know how humiliating that is for a five year old?! She reminded me that white was always right and black is lower than the dirt between my toes! I hated that woman with every bone in my body," Pauline shouted so loud, she shook like a palm tree in winter.

Tawny splayed a hand over her chest and gasped like she'd seen a ghost. Samuel placed his hands on Pauline's shoulders and squeezed them gently. Tawny tried to compose herself and pursed her lips together like she was disappointed at Pauline's shocking words.

"You can't help that you inherited my butterscotch complexion, but you know that Lillian did all she could to help me by babysitting you while I was at work. No, she wasn't the greatest person in the world, but she was the greatest at what she did," Tawny exclaimed. "I never told you this before, but um, when your grandma Lillian was on her death bed, she told me that you were a very beautiful baby, but if you were lighter you'd be more beautiful. She apologized to me about the way she treated you, right before she took her last breath," Tawny's eyes glistened and her lips trembled to unlock the rest of the words in her mouth. "She asked me if I could find it in my heart to forgive her and told me to name my future grandchild after her and then she shut her eyes for good." Tawny blotted her eyes with a napkin and sniffled.

Pauline wasn't fazed by the dramatics, so she clapped her hands like she was at a Broadway show. "Bravo,

Mother, bravo. I guess you've yet to realize that I didn't name my first born after her. What makes you think I'm going to name my second born after her?" Pauline furiously asked.

Samuel was in awe and he looked like he wanted to say something, but he was having a hard time searching for the next thing to say. Too many shocking revelations were hitting him from each direction at once, so he continued rubbing Pauline's shoulders. Pauline rolled her eyes and sat away from Samuel a little. Samuel knew that the whole scene wasn't taking a good turn, so he moved closer to Pauline in hopes of diffusing the brewing tension in the room. He normally would have dropped his two cents into their disagreement, but he had other things that were harassing his spirit. "Sweetie, calm down. Remember what the doctor said, okay?" Samuel gently said and resumed massaging her shoulders.

Pauline gave him a knowing look, pulled away from him again and stood up this time. "Samuel, I know exactly what the doctor said. I'm just voicing my opinions about my grandma Lillian, the racist."

Tawny gently placed her cup of tea on the table, stood up and gave Pauline an evil glare. "My dear, I understand how upsetting this is to you, but you can't go around carrying hatred for your grandma in your heart. You must forgive her for your own good or you're going to end up bitter, and God will never forgive you. Lillian made peace with me before she went on to glory and you should do the same, young lady." Tawny scolded Pauline like she was a child again.

Pauline squinted her eyes and folded her arms. "Are you listening to yourself? You're acting like I should forget it ever happened."

"As a matter of fact, I think you should, because you can't undo the past. What's done is done, and there's nothing you can do about it, except move on," Tawny said matter-of-factly and sat back down.

"Oh, so I guess it would be okay for Sylvester's daughter to pretend that he never molested her either. Is that right?" Pauline shot back.

Tawny shot up from her seat and she shook her finger at Pauline. "I beg your pardon? I will not sit here and listen to you disrespect your fa—"

"Stepfather! He's my stepfather and that's all he'll ever be!" Pauline angrily corrected.

Tawny gasped and clutched her chest like she was about to have a coronary attack. "I don't know what's gotten into you, but I will not tolerate that type of tone or talk, young lady. I am still your mother!" Tawny scolded and shook her finger at Pauline.

"Well, then, you need to start acting more like my mother than some righteous Catholic school teacher. You never find fault in anyone when they're in the wrong, especially when it comes to Sylvester."

"Now, you wait one min—"

"No, I'm still talking. Let me say what I have to say, okay?" Pauline sternly stated and held her finger up to silence her mother.

Samuel found it funny that Pauline was criticizing her mother for defending people who were in the wrong when she repeatedly did the same thing she was accusing her mother of.

"Sylvester has been great to us, but he's no saint. He may have prayed and repented for what he did and God may have forgiven him, but he can't undo what he's done to his own daughter. Doreen's going to spend the rest of life living with some of the most troubling childhood memories of her life, and I think the last thing she wants to do is pretend that being molested by her own father never existed. We all can forgive and forget, but old memories can be triggered and they can spill all over our minds and bodies like an incurable disease. Forgiveness isn't easy and neither should it be expected overnight. For people like Sylvester, forgiveness should be a privilege, not a right."

There was dead silence for a split second. Then Tawny cleared her voice and pursed her lips together once again and gave Pauline an icy cold stare. "Well, I guess I missed the memo, because I had no idea that Jesus had died and left you as spokesperson for forgiveness and judgment," Tawny derisively said and folded her arms.

"Mother, that is blasphemy."

"Ha! So not only are you accusing me of being forgiving, but you're accusing me of disrespecting God. May I remind you that before you married Samuel, you were just another college dropout who was just shy of becoming a stripper at Big Daddy's Doll House?" Tawny derisively said.

Pauline flinched a little and her lips curled. Tawny had struck a chord in Pauline that sent shock waves to her brain, invoking those distasteful memories. "You didn't have to go there, Mother. That was a long time ago. It's not like I became a pregnant teen. And as much as I love you, I felt like I could never speak to you about the things that were troubling me, because you always found something to criticize me about. I wanted to become a model, but you told me that I wasn't skinny enough and that the modeling industry would devour me to nothing. When I told you I wanted to become a dentist, you told me that it was a dirty job and the only job I'd be fit to do was secretarial work. You always found the smallest flaw in me, and enlarged it. Sometimes I would ask God why you hated me so much and why I couldn't do anything right." Pauline's face tightened, and tears started sliding down her cheeks.

Tawny's face softened as she cupped her mouth and tried to embrace Pauline, but Pauline stepped out of her reach. Tawny stopped in her tracks and gave her daughter a pitiful look. "Oh, sweetheart…I am so sorry. I had no idea that you felt that way. I know we didn't always have the best relationship, but you know I always wanted what was best for you. That's why I pushed you the way I did because I wanted you to become a better woman than I was. But—"

"Go ahead and say it: I disappointed you and disgraced the family," Pauline angrily said.

"No, darling. I mean, yes, instead of finishing college you decided to marry a pastor's son who's now a rich televangelist, but at least you don't have to struggle and scrounge for everything like I did when I was raising you. Besides, when you met and married Samuel, you became a better woman," Tawny said and forced a smile.

Pauline shook her head and smiled to halt the racing tears. "Way to go, Mother. If I didn't know any better, I'd think you were trying to call me a gold digger. There's just no getting through to you, huh?"

"See, there you go jumping to conclusions like you always do. You are just as bullheaded as your father."

"If you're alluding to my real father, you're right about the bullheadedness. He was bullheaded because you made him that way. It explains why he drank the way he did. You're the one who constantly belittled him for not being able to find a job when he came back from the military. He didn't die because he drank so much. He died from the broken heart you gave him!"

"How can you say something so terrible? Do you have any idea how much crap I had to put up with from your father? Your father drank so much, he would call me everything but my name, and he would tear up the house. So I did what I had to do for my protection and yours. Whenever—"

"Bull crap! One night when you thought I was asleep, I overheard you telling Daddy that he was worthless, and because he was unable to find a job and take care of us like a real man, you ended up screwing his creepy looking childhood best friend, one-eyed Pete! Yeah, you didn't think I ever knew about that, did you?" Pauline challenged.

Tawny held onto her chair out of fear of falling out, but she remained calm. "Yes, I did make love to his best friend," she conceded. "He may have had only one good eye, but he always made sure that you and I never wanted for anything. He never criticized me, he made me feel like a woman, and he always treated me like a lady. He also never walked around feeling sorry for himself the way your father did. Hell, your father came back from the war unscathed and unharmed and he complained about everything, even if it was a tiny piece of lint on the carpet. Not only was one-eyed Pete good to me, but he had a penis that could make a nun lose her religion. Your daddy lost his thunder in the bedroom and he also lost my respect. I was tired of being his mule, so I did what I thought was best for me and you. Therefore, I don't feel like I owe you or anyone an explanation. Is that clear?" Tawny said with authority and straightened her posture.

"It's very clear. It's very clear that you only did what you thought was best for you. It is also clear that you destroyed Daddy's lifelong friendship with one-eyed Pete by spreading your legs like some common harlot."

Tawny gasped again. "Are you calling me a harlot?"

"If the slutty red dress fits, wear it," Pauline calmly said.

Tawny slapped Pauline, but she didn't flinch. Instead, she stood there motionless and smirked. Samuel was shocked beyond words. "Feels great, doesn't it, Mother? That's the same way Father slapped you when you told him that one-eyed Pete's love marathon was better than his two minute warm-ups. You know, it's funny how you prance around the house like you're the black Martha Stewart who never committed a sin. I mean, you cheated on my father and now you're married to Sylvester, the child molester." Pauline smirked again, and stared her mother up and down in disdain.

Samuel finally intervened. "Ladies, please."

"You know what, Pauline? If I'd known you'd behave this way, I wouldn't have invited you. Better yet, I'd rather you leave, because I have no idea who you are, and I refuse to be disrespected in my own house. Samuel, I'm sorry you had to witness all of this." Tawny reached for her napkin and began blowing her nose as she wept softly.

"Mom, Pauline didn't mean what she said. You two obviously have a lot to talk about. I do family counseling all the time, and we'll do a session whenever you two are ready," Samuel said while continuously rubbing Pauline's shoulders.

"I'm afraid that won't be necessary, Samuel. It seems that my daughter has pretty much made her mind up about me and her stepfather. Excuse me; I need to be alone," Tawny said between weeps and wiped her face.

"Mom, please stay. We can work this out," Samuel sympathetically said.

"No, my daughter hates me," Tawny wailed and stormed up the stairs.

"Mom, please," Samuel begged again and tried to follow Tawny to stop her.

"Let her go. She'll be okay," Pauline dismissively waved and rolled her eyes. "Besides, it's about time someone popped her perfect little bubble. She always acts like she's some black Judy Cleaver or something. She thinks she's better than people when she's already put a nasty taste in Jesus' mouth with her unsavory past." Pauline took a seat on the sofa and crossed her legs with a look of disappointment on her face.

"Baby, you really surprise me. I've never heard you speak to your mother that way before and I had no idea you felt that way about her. You always try to be the voice of reason and now this. I had no idea that she'd messed around on your father. How come you never told me all of this? I'm really sorry, baby. I still think I should go see if your mother is alright," Samuel said. He grabbed Pauline's hand and squeezed it gently.

Moments later, Sylvester entered the house with a dazzling smile on his face. He looked like he'd just returned from a ball instead of doing his missionary work. The tuxedo he wore made him look like a lanky penguin. He was a wiry built man with the complexion of sandalwood. He was fairly handsome with dimples so deep, they looked like punctures in his cheeks; tiny moles crowded the corners of his eyes, and a pencil-thin mustache and Caesar haircut completed his appearance. He was holding brown bags of groceries.

"Hello, my beautiful people. It's so great to see you all on this beautiful morning in the name of Jesus," he said with zeal.

Samuel and Pauline were caught off guard. "Hey, um, how are you?" Samuel said and cleared his throat.

Pauline immediately got up to greet Sylvester. Sylvester placed the bags on the floor to embrace her. "It's so good to see you, Daddy," Pauline happily said and embraced him.

"The feeling is mutual, baby girl. I've missed you so much," Sylvester said, returning the embrace.

Samuel sat there speechless and confused. Isn't this the same woman who just got done bashing Sylvester and called him a child molester? And now she's embracing him like she never had a bad thing to say about him. This is some crazy ass mess! he thought.

Sylvester gently pulled away from Pauline and gave her a once over. "My, my, my. Look at how beautiful you look. Girl, I swear you get more beautiful by the second. And how is our little angel doing?" Sylvester said and rubbed her belly.

"He or she is doing well. I can't wait to meet him or her." Pauline rubbed her belly.

"And where's Chastity?"

"Um, well, didn't Mother tell you?" Pauline hesitantly said.

"Tell me what?" Sylvester incredulously asked.

Samuel poured in his two cents. "We didn't want to take Chastity out of school for so many days and our nanny Etta Rose insisted on watching her while we're away because she loves her like a granddaughter," Samuel said and smiled uncomfortably.

"Oh, I see," Sylvester said with hurt in his eyes.

"But Chastity did tell us to tell you she said hello," Pauline quickly said.

"She sure did," Samuel said and placed his shaky hands in his pockets.

"I was counting on seeing her; I'm surprised Tawny never told me that my precious Chastity wasn't going to be here. It's such a shame, because I had a little surprise for her." Sylvester sighed, shook his head, and collected the bags of groceries.

"Let me help you with that," Pauline offered.

"No, baby girl. You and Samuel go and have a seat. You're our guests. Besides, I'd already planned to make you all some waffles, sausage, eggs, and cheese grits. And now that you're eating for two, I made sure to buy plenty of food," Sylvester said with a wink. "By the way, where's your mother?" he asked.

"She's upstairs in her room. She should be down momentarily," Pauline answered with uncertainty.

"Honey, I'm home," Sylvester shouted and headed into the kitchen.

Pauline gave Samuel an admonishing look. "Samuel, I want you to be on your best behavior and I'm going to do the same thing. I don't want Sylvester finding out about what just happened. We're just going to act like everything is normal, okay?" Pauline nervously said and straightened out her dress.

Samuel gave her a side-eyed look. "If you say so."

"I'm serious, Samuel. If Sylvester finds out about our little exchange, we're going to have a lot of explaining to do; he's a very sensitive man."

Samuel furrowed his eyebrows. "Little exchange is an understatement. You have that poor woman upstairs crying her eyes out after calling her a harlot."

Pauline shot Samuel a poisonous look that could have laid him to rest. "Oh, so now it's my fault? Whose side are you on, Samuel?" Pauline defensively asked.

"I'm not on anyone's side, but you have to admit that you laid your mother's transgressions on her thicker than beeswax. I mean, I understand your frustrations, but you didn't hold back either."

"I see. So, I'm wrong for pointing out her worldly past because she hurt me, right?"

"See, there you go putting words in my mouth. All I'm saying is—"

"Save it, Samuel. I've heard enough," Pauline retorted, held her palm up to Samuel's face, stood and walked away.

Samuel sighed. "And where are you going?" Samuel asked in a dry tone.

"To the kitchen; is that alright with you?" Pauline hissed and continued toward the kitchen.

Samuel shook his head and sighed again. That damn woman gets more stubborn and bipolar by the millimeter of a second. It must be the pregnancy hormones settling in. But then again, she never behaved this way when she was pregnant with Chastity. Women; can't live with them, can't live without 'em. Samuel chuckled to himself. Then he thought about Tawny and realized it was the perfect opportunity to go check on her. He heard Pauline and Sylvester bantering in the kitchen, obviously catching up on lost time. Samuel quickly trotted up the stairs. He didn't know which bedroom Tawny was in. There were two bedroom doors on the right and he saw one bedroom door on the left. Then he heard faint sniffling resonating from the second room on the right. He slowly approached the door and lightly knocked on it. Samuel heard Tawny whimpering.

"Mom, it's me, Samuel," Samuel said as he knocked on the door.

"Who is it?" Tawny replied in a throaty tone.

"It's Samuel," he repeated.

"I'll be out momentarily. I just need some time alone for now," she said and blew her nose. It sounded like a trumpet.

"I know, but I am a little worried about you. Is it okay if I come in?" Samuel asked while slowly turning the door knob.

"You don't have to worry about me. Why don't you go downstairs and join Pauline and Sylvester. I'll be downstairs, okay?" Tawny said and sniffled once more.

"No, because I believe you're saying that just to get me out of your hair. Well, I am not leaving until you open this door, Mom," Samuel defiantly said.

Tawny sighed and shook her head. "Come in," she uttered.

Samuel entered the room and gently closed the door behind him. His heart nearly sank into his pants pocket when saw Tawny sitting on the edge of the bed blotting her red, puffy eyes.

"How can she be so self-centered? After everything I've done for her. It just isn't fair," Tawny complained and blew her nose once more.

Samuel stood near the antique chest in the room, because he thought it would be awkward to sit next to her on her bed. Tawny's room was adorned with lavender colors. Everything, from the drapes on the window to the plush carpet, was lavender and boasted a woman's touch.

"I'm sure Pauline didn't mean what she said. Between you and me, she had nothing but nice things to say about Sylvester before we got here. It's probably her pregnancy hormones. So, I'm sure she didn't mean it," Samuel said with reassurance.

Tawny looked at Samuel like he'd sprouted horns on his head, grew fangs, and was hoisting a pitch fork. "She did? Then how come she said I wasn't supportive to her and her father? I fought tooth and nail to make sure she had the best clothes, education, and home. Believe me Samuel, I tried the very best I could to raise Pauline so that she wouldn't end up another fallen woman, or struggle to stretch pennies the way I did. She owes me an apology!" Tawny shouted and shook her fist.

Samuel suddenly took a seat next to Tawny and put his arm around her shoulder. "Mom, you've done well with Pauline. You and I both know that. But you haven't taken the time to give her the benefit of the doubt. Have you considered how she feels, or tried to understand what it's like to not be taken seriously or be shut out when you tell someone what your passions and goals are? I can personally attest to how Pauline feels because honestly, I never planned to become a pastor. I only chose to become a pastor because my father would have it no other way. I aspired to become a paramedic."

"Oh my," Tawny said with a burst of surprise. "But Samuel, you're good at what you do. You're a multi-millionaire, for Christ's sakes. You've accomplished more than some people ever would in a hundred life times. Your father knew what was best for you and he was right. I mean, look how affluent and well-respected you are. You're a prolific man with a lifestyle that many people would die for. Now, on the other hand, Pauline has always been wishy-washy. The child could barely endorse a check. She didn't always get the best grades and she always wanted to do whatever she wanted to do. I had to do what I knew was best for her because I knew if I allowed her to make her own decisions, they would result in a calamity and that, sir, is a no-no. At times she could be so darn stubborn. That's something she inherited from her father. Sometimes I don't know what to do with that child," Tawny said in a quivering tear-drenched tone.

"And that's where you keep going wrong," said Samuel.

"What do you mean?" Tawny suspiciously asked with her eyebrows furrowed.

"You abused your authority as a parent by not allowing Pauline to exercise her freedom as an individual."

"Come again? I allowed Pauline to have a social life, but she hung out with kids I didn't like."

"And what did you not like about them?"

"Well, some of the girls she hung out with wore mini-skirts and heavy make-up. They looked like 3rd class prostitutes. There was no way I was going to allow Pauline to hang out with those kinds of people—period," Tawny said and defiantly folded her arms.

"You do have a point, but what about when Pauline said she came to you about her career endeavors; she said you would say negative things about why she shouldn't pursue them. Yes, she made some bad decisions, but at least she tried to do something productive and you didn't give her the benefit of the doubt," Samuel reminded.

The tears in Tawny's eyes spilled out again. "I don't understand this. Now you're siding with her. Now you're accusing me of not mothering my daughter

properly. I never expected this from you, Samuel."
Tawny cried so hard she hiccupped.

Samuel sighed and put his hand on her knee. "I love you, Mom and I am not taking anyone's side. However, I am not speaking to you as your son-in-law right now. I am speaking to you as a family counselor who cares and loves you as well. You and Pauline both hate to recognize your faults, but the only way you two are going to come to a mutual understanding is when you speak to each other about it. You two obviously have a lot on your chest that you need to release. Adults air out their grievances so they can move on. This is the only way you and Pauline will be able to patch up your differences."

"Well...I-I-I," Tawny stammered and trailed off. "I guess you're right. The only way Pauline and I will move forward is if we acknowledge where we went wrong and put it behind us," Tawny said and exhaled a little. "I love her very much and I don't want anything coming between us. I thank you for stopping by and giving me a dose of reality. Sylvester is always telling me how stubborn I am," Tawny conceded and hung her head in shame.

"Ya think?" Samuel chuckled. "You and Pauline are both very stubborn, but Sylvester and I love and cherish you two to smithereens," he said and gave Tawny a hug.

"Aww, I know, son," Tawny said and returned the affection with a kiss on the cheek. "You have an innate gift for simplifying things that are so difficult. My daughter is lucky to have a husband like you."

"I can't take all the credit. It's God who works through me."

"You can say that again," Tawny chuckled.

"I also think it would be a great idea to add Sylvester to the counseling session as well, but not until you and Pauline work the kinks out of your relationship, though. It might make everything seem less awkward," Samuel suggested with surprise on his face. He personally didn't care for Sylvester but then he realized it couldn't hurt. Plus, it would give him the opportunity to confirm if Sylvester was really a changed man who wouldn't revert back to being a child molester.

"I don't know. I mean, Sylvester is a proud man and he's repented for his sins, but he can be stubborn as a horse, too," Tawny said in an uncertain tone and shook her head.

"Well, you can ask him about being part of the session. You don't have to mention anything about his past and we'll let it flow easily."

"I'll see what I can do," Tawny said with a sigh.

"It's going to be okay, Mom."

"I hope so."

"It will," Samuel affirmed. Tawny's smile returned to her face. "We'd better go meet them in the kitchen before they begin looking for us," Samuel said.

"Good idea," Tawny said and nodded in agreement. "I'm going to go clean my face, then I'll meet you in the kitchen."

"Okay, I'll see you there." Samuel got up to make his exit.

"Oh, and, Samuel," Tawny said.

"Yes?" he replied as he pulled open the door.

"Thank you."

"Don't mention it," Samuel said with a wink and closed the door.

As soon as he exited the room, his nose was greeted by the savory aroma from the food in the kitchen. He quickly descended the stairs and trotted into the kitchen to join Sylvester and Pauline.

"Hey you," he said and gave Pauline a peck on the cheek.

She was caught off guard. "Heeey," she slowly said with a half-smile. "It took you long enough." She popped a grape into her mouth.

"Oh, well, um…" Samuel hadn't prepared himself for what he was going to say next. And he knew Pauline wasn't going to let him get off the hook that easily, either. Thankfully, Tawny came into the kitchen to save him from interrogation in the nick of time.

"Hello, everyone," Tawny said in a cheery tone. "Mmm, I am loving the aroma. Boy, that husband of mine is a fine cook, isn't he?" she added and pulled herself a seat. Sylvester winked at her and continued cooking up a storm.

There was still tension between Pauline and Tawny that was so foggy, you could draw letters through it. Tawny was the first person to break the shroud between them. "Pauline, I'd like to apologize for the way I behaved earlier and you're right; I have been too hard on you and I hope you find it in your heart to forgive me."

"Thank you," was all Pauline said without giving Tawny any eye contact.

Tawny looked at Samuel with pity in her eyes. Samuel looked at her and gave her a thumbs up for effort.

"Sorry about what?" Sylvester asked while looking over his shoulder at the three of them.

"Oh, it's nothing," Tawny said with a wave of her hand. "Pauline and I had a little disagreement earlier about what we should name the baby, but we've come to an agreement. Right, honey?" Tawny responded with a faux smile.

Pauline didn't say anything and popped another grape into her mouth, with complete annoyance written on her face. "First, you apologize to me, and now you expect me to lie. Ha! What a hoot!" Pauline said with a sardonic laugh.

"Pauline, that isn't fair," Tawny sadly said.

"What isn't fair is that you still want to play the victim after apologizing. You're always playing the victim!"

"Calm down, Pauline," Samuel said and tried to stand in between her and Tawny. "Calm down, my behind! I am getting tired of you defending this poor excuse for a mother and woman!" she shouted.

"Ladies, ladies, calm down. It's too early in the morning to bicker and I'm preparing us a wonderful meal," Sylvester said, showing them the skillet of sizzling pork bacon as a white flag to settle the dispute.

"You stay out of this, Sylvester! And you too, Samuel! As a matter of fact, I'm not hungry. I've just lost my appetite. Excuse me," Pauline huffed and left the kitchen.

"What's the matter with her?" Sylvester asked, giving Samuel and Tawny a confounded look. Tawny sat there quietly and tapped her fingers on the table. "Will someone please tell me what's going on?" Sylvester insisted.

"It's nothing, Sylvester. Pauline is having another one of her mood swings again. You know how pregnant women get." The fake smile on her face was convincing but her words weren't convincing enough.

Sylvester didn't believe her. "No, something is wrong," Sylvester said while placing the skillet back on the stove and turning down the fire. "When she was in the kitchen, she didn't say much to me but she wasn't unfriendly either. I figured she was kind of tired from her pregnancy, but when you entered the kitchen and started talking to her, she became a whole other person."

Tawny hesitated and looked at Samuel for backup.

"Like you said, Sylvester, she's just tired," Samuel added.

"Hmm...then why did she just walk out of the kitchen in a funk? I understand that people have their differences, but whatever Tawny and Pauline were discussing didn't take a great turn. I've known Pauline almost her whole life and I know when something is or isn't right. I need one of you to explain to me what's going on." Sylvester gave both of them an accusatory look and furrowed his eyebrows. "I can smell a rat." His eyes shifted from Tawny to Samuel and back to Tawny.

Samuel cleared his throat once again to figure out his next excuse. "You know how Pauline is. She's pregnant and she's moody. She can be unpredictable at times. I wouldn't worry so much about her," Samuel said with a smile and looked to Tawny for rescue. Thankfully, she picked up where he'd left off and he was hoping she'd put a better spin on his version and lay Sylvester's suspicions to rest.

"Yes, um, Samuel's right. Pauline is stressed and her pregnancy is tiring her out. That's why she went upstairs to rest because she gets cranky when she doesn't get enough sleep. No biggie." Tawny feigned another smile and stood closer to Samuel to sort of break the thickening tension in the room; she hoped she wasn't obvious.

"Hmm…then why are your eyes kind of red," Sylvester pointed out.

We're busted. This child molesting bastard is smarter than we give him credit for! Samuel thought with the same surprised look that a child had when they were caught putting their hands in a cookie jar.

Tawny fidgeted with her bun and stammered over her words. "Oh, um, well, dust got into my eyes. That's all." She looked at Samuel and maintained her phony smile. The tension was getting so thick that it could have suffocated all three of them.

Sylvester folded his arms and scanned both of their faces in more depth. "I don't know what kind of fool you two take me for. And I'm not going to stand here and continue playing this guessing game with you, either. You two are obviously hiding something, and Tawny, I know you and my baby girl got into it. I'm going to go upstairs and get to the bottom of this," Sylvester angrily said.

"Sylvester, don't. Pauline needs her rest," Tawny said while trying to stop Sylvester from going upstairs. "We can talk about this over breakfast."

"No, I'm going to speak to my daughter because since you two want to tiptoe around the tulips, she'll tell me everything I need to know."

"But, dear, she needs her rest. Can you at least wait until she gets up?" Tawny implored and grabbed his arm.

"Listen, I'm going upstairs to talk to my daughter, not interrogate her. I still have that right, don't I?" Sylvester angrily asked and pulled away from Tawny.

"Sylv—"

"I've heard enough, Tawny. I'm going to talk to my daughter and that's that," Sylvester shouted, causing Tawny to jump and accidentally bite her tongue.

She could taste the salty blood and she rubbed her tongue around the inside of her mouth to stop the pain and bleeding. Then she looked at Samuel to come to her aid. That's when he finally intervened.

"Tawny, I mean, Mother is right. Pauline needs her rest. Tell you what; I'll go get her," Samuel offered.

"Listen, boy; she's my daughter and I will go talk to my daughter anytime I want. So why don't the both of you stay here and have some breakfast, okay?" Sylvester snapped.

Tawny gasped and covered her mouth. "How dare you speak to Samuel that way?" she uttered

"I can speak to whomever, however I want to in my own house," Sylvester said and shot Samuel a wicked glare that could turn water into ice.

No this bastard didn't, Samuel thought but he kept his composure. "With all due respect, Pauline is your stepdaughter, but she's still my wife. Besides, Mom is right. Pauline needs her rest and we shouldn't be adding to her stress and anxiety by nagging her about little stuff. Pauline and Tawny just had a little misunderstanding about what to name the baby."

Sylvester furrowed his eyebrows once more. "Son, I've heard a bunch of poppycock in my days, but this one takes the icing and cherry off the cake. Now, if you'll excuse me, I'm going to—" Sylvester stopped mid-sentence and froze like a mannequin when Pauline entered the kitchen.

"What's all of the commotion about?" she asked with a perplexed look on her face.

"Pauline, dear. Have a seat. Your father and I were just talking about you. Are you feeling better now?" Tawny replied with a nervous smile.

"What's going on in here?" Pauline incredulously inquired. A moment of silence impregnated the room and the only thing that could be heard in the kitchen was the water dripping from the sink faucet. "Will someone please tell me what's going on?!" Pauline shouted.

"Um, sweetheart, if something is bothering you, you can always talk to us," Sylvester said as he grabbed Pauline's hand and rubbed it. "What's the matter?" he asked.

"I'm fine. I just want a glass of water," Pauline irritatingly replied and gently pulled away from Sylvester. Before Sylvester could utter his next set of questions, he caught Samuel giving him a firm look. "Sure, a glass of water coming up," he said and went to take a glass out of the sink.

"I want bottled water. I never drink tap water because it contains all sorts of toxins and chlorine," Pauline said as she sat down.

"Oh, yeah, right. Bottled water coming right up," Sylvester said, sounding like Isaac Washington in "The Love Boat". Sylvester looked in the refrigerator and scanned its content for water. "Sweetheart, we're out of bottled water. But we do have some orange juice, tea, sod—"

"I don't want orange juice, because it gives me gas. I usually only drink green tea; I had sweet tea earlier when we first arrived. Soda makes me break out and it's detrimental to the kidneys. I guess I'll die from dehydration before there will ever be any bottled water replenished in this house," Pauline hissed and started to leave the table.

Tawny and Sylvester had helpless looks on their faces. Samuel was the only one who spoke. "I'll drive to the store and buy some water. Is there anything else I can get you, sweetheart?" Samuel asked calmly.

Pauline paused for a moment. "I'll have a huge jar of pickles, cheese doodles, glazed donuts, and pistachio ice cream."

"Goodness grief, dear. It's early in the morning and—" Tawny started.

"And that is what Pauline shall have because she's eating for two now. Right, baby?" Samuel interrupted and gave Tawny a knowing look.

"Sure, yes, it's whatever Pauline wants," Tawny corrected herself and cleared her throat.

"Right," Sylvester chimed in.

"I'm going upstairs. Excuse me," Pauline solemnly said and disappeared.

"How can you let your wife eat all of that garbage? She's turning her uterus into a landfield for our unborn granddaughter," Tawny complained.

"Let her have whatever she wants. Now, I see why you two didn't want me to speak to her. I have never seen my baby girl so upset, and I trust that she will not over indulge on junk food. I mean, look at Chastity; she's healthy as a bull," Sylvester finally said.

"Relax, you two. I will get Pauline something so deliciously nutritious that she will forget about all of those unhealthy snacks she requested," Samuel said.

"And how can you be so sure?" Tawny incredulously asked and placed a hand on her curvy hip.

"Because I'm Pastor Samuel Lee Baker, the one and only," Samuel boasted with confidence and winked.

～～　～～

"Did you get all the other items I told you to get?" Pauline asked without looking up at Samuel as she sifted through a Vanity Fair magazine.

"Better. Here, open it up," Samuel said with a smile and handed her a pink envelope with a purple bow on it.

When she opened the envelope, she saw a gift card and gasped. It was a $15,000 gift card to Saks Fifth Avenue. Pauline began to tear up. "Samuel, you shouldn't have!!" She gave him a huge hug, and kissed him all over his face. Samuel laughed between kisses."I'm sorry about the way I behaved earlier. I shouldn't have acted that way. I owe all of you an apology."

"It's okay. We understand and we still love you."

"I still feel guilty about how I acted and spoke to you all earlier. I wish there was a way I could make it up to my parents," Pauline sadly said with shame nesting in her eyes.

"We'll both figure that out and that won't be hard to do, either. But in the meantime, you can make it up to me right now," Samuel said and wrapped her into his arms, smiling mischievously at her.

"You already know, big papa," Pauline giggled and planted a big wet kiss on his lips.

"Mmmm…I love it when ya call me big papa!" Samuel said and they both laughed and made long passionate love like never before.

~ ~   ~ ~

Tawny was still upset by what happened between her and Pauline and she wanted to bury the hatchet. What bothered her more was when Pauline mentioned Doreen being molested by Sylvester. Tawny knew that Sylvester had turned over a new leaf—or so she told herself. She lived in utter denial about Sylvester being a child molester; she knew that Doreen had never reported him to the authorities, but she was sure Doreen would never forgive him. What Tawny never admitted to Pauline was that she'd actually seen naked pictures of a teenage Doreen. Tawny thought back to when she'd first met Sylvester.

When Tawny had first met Sylvester, it had been love at first sight. She met him at Mt. Sinai Methodist Church in Virginia and he was one of the deacons. She'd caught a flat in her tire after church service and didn't have a spare tire, so he'd helped her replace the damaged tire with one of his spare tires. When she got a good look at him, there was something about him that made her swoon and soon after, they'd begun dating. Whenever they attended church, Tawny would hear some of the other church members snicker, whisper, talk behind her back, and give her funny looks. Instead of reacting, she let all the gossip roll off her back like sweat.

That was until three thugs busted through the church on motorcycles during a wedding service. The guests were scared motionless. The thugs identified themselves as members of Satan's Angels gang. They were the black version of Hell's Angels. They all wore black leather and the back of their jackets had a picture of a winged, brown skull with blood dripping from its sockets. The emblem of their name Satan's Angels was outlined in red to resemble blood and it was scribed above the skull.

The ring leader, who was about 6 feet 5 inches, removed his helmet to reveal a long beard that was formed into one fat, long, matted loc, that touched his pregnant-looking belly; he was the size of a mountain. He wore a shag at the center of his bald head that consisted of one long free-form loc that hung past his butt and he wore a pair of Rayban shades. When he got off his bike, he asked for Sylvester. Sylvester emerged from his seat and raised his hand. He trembled and was afraid he was going to die at that very moment.

Tawny was bewildered. "Baby, what are you doing?" she nervously asked Sylvester.

"It's okay, baby. I can handle this; just stay where you are, okay?" Sylvester said to her with fear in his voice.

Franklin Milford who was the church's pastor at the time. He was petrified and so was the choir. The bride and groom were also frightened beyond belief.

"I-I-I am Sylvester, um, sir, mister sir," Sylvester stuttered and trembled.

Pastor Milford intervened. "Young man, we're in the middle of a wedding. What is your business with Sylvester?"

The ring leader removed his shades to reveal one eye and stared Pastor Milford in the face. Pastor Milford buckled like a horse that was being branded. The bride burst into tears and the groom shielded her in his arms. The ring leader blew the bride a kiss and she cried out once more. The groom gave the ring leader a disgusted look but he didn't dare say what was on his mind. The ring leader redirected his attention to Pastor Milford and Sylvester.

"My business with this sick ass nigga here is that he's been pokin' his dick in my woman, Doreen," the ringleader said, as he pointed his finger at Sylvester.

"I beg your pardon, young man? Sylvester would do no such thing and you are in the house of the Lord. You will refrain from using that type of language. I'm afraid I must ask you to leave," Pastor Milford said in a trembling voice.

The ring leader laughed and looked at his crew who also laughed, then he suddenly reached inside of his jacket and pulled out an ice pick. Before he confronted Sylvester, he warned the rest of the people in the church. "If any of you muthafuckas in here don't want a multiple funeral in here, you'd better not call the pigs, because my boys are strapped with AK-47s."

His henchmen revealed their guns to make their threats loud and clear. The bride cried out again, and the helpless groom could do nothing but console her. None of the other folks dared challenge those thugs. They were outraged, but they kept their thoughts and cries amongst each other. It was almost like they were in a concentration camp instead of a wedding. Tawny was also crying.

"Bring your punk ass over here, bitch!" the ring leader ordered.

"Please don't hurt me, sir," Sylvester begged with a gesture of surrender as he took baby steps toward the ring leader.

The ring leader charged at Sylvester, snatched him up by his collar and held the sharp ice pick at Sylvester's chest.

"Oh my God, sweet Jesus!" Tawny cried out and fell to her knees. "Please don't hurt my fiancé!"

"Yo, Mark," the ring leader said.

"Yeah, Mangy."

"Come shut this bitch up for me."

235

"Alright," Mark said in a nonchalant tone. Terrorizing law-biding citizens was the norm for Mark because he didn't flinch about anything that was graphic or disturbing. Mark removed his brown bandanna from around his head and swiftly approached Tawny.

"No, please don't hurt me," she said in a terrified tone.

Mark ignored her, swiftly grabbed her into a choke hold and forced his bandanna into her mouth. She nearly choked and cried a little.

"Please don't hurt my fiancée," Sylvester desperately pleaded.

"Shut yo' punk ass up," Mangy barked and punched Sylvester in the face, sending him to the floor. He was out cold.

"Somebody call the police!" shouted a light-skinned wiry woman.

Mark, and Mangy's other henchman, Terror, who was the size of a sumo wrestler, drew their guns at the crowd, infecting more fear into them like a flu-shot.

"I wouldn't try that if I was y'all. If you don't want this wedding to end up a funeral, I suggest y'all act like none of this ever happened," Mangy said while pointing his gun at a frightened woman who turned into the color of a red onion and fainted.

The entire scene seemed to unfold in slow motion and nothing could be heard but heartbeats. Pastor Milford finally spoke up. "Young man, we don't want any trouble," he said in a trembling voice. "If there's anything you want, just let me know. I'm sure there are other ways we can settle this like men. Please put the gun down. You're scaring everyone," Pastor Milford continued with glistening eyes.

Mangy shot Pastor Milford a wicked look. His eyes darted to Sylvester lying on the floor in a limp-like manner and then he yanked him from the floor like a mannequin and stood him up to face him. "Hold your hand up, nigga," Mangy commanded.

Pastor Milford watched the unfolding scene in horror. Samuel reluctantly did what Mangy instructed him to do. Mangy effortlessly drove the ice pick into Sylvester's hand, causing blood to squirt out of it. Terror laughed like he was at a Kevin Hart concert. Tawny yelped and that's when Mark grabbed her into another choke hold like her going to break her neck.

"You'd better not scream or we'll do you worse than your old man, dig?" Mark seethed and smacked her across the head.

237

"Damn right," Mangy said. He gave Mark a high five and they both laughed it off.

Sylvester was in so much pain, he thought he was going into shock.

Pastor Milford wailed and came to Sylvester's rescue. Samuel's hand was covered in so much blood, it looked like he was wearing a red leather glove. Pastor Milford looked at Mangy with a plea in his eyes and said, "Please, young man. I am sure if there's anything you want, we'll give it to ya. We don't want any trouble. You have proven your point."

Mangy chuckled and pulled a cigar out of his leather jacket pocket and lit it. He took a hard pull on the cigar, pensively stared at the ceiling and then he flicked the ashes on Sylvester and and the pastor. Pastor Milford coughed and waved off the smoke that threatened to invade his nostrils.

"Tell ya what. I want you to write me a check for $100,000 and ol' bitch boy is never ever to have any kind of contact with my ol' lady, or the next time, I won't be so nice," Mangy said in a menacing tone.

Pastor Milford gulped so loud, he almost choked on it. "Okay, we'll give you what you want. You're scaring everyone and you made your point. Please leave," he begged in a cowering position.

Mangy continued taking long drags on his cigar. Then he towered over Sylvester. "Dude just saved your life, bitch boy. I ain't one for issuin' warnings to niggas. I usually do them in. But I'll say this; if I find out you tryin' to get in contact with my ol' lady by phone or in person, I'm gonna turn your ass into a memory before you even get a chance to hang up the phone or walk out the door. Am I clear, nigga?" Mangy bellowed in a menacing tone.

All Sylvester could do was yelp like a wounded moose on the highway. Mangy didn't hesitate to kick Sylvester in the small of his back with his leather black cowboy boot. "Yeeesss!" Sylvester cried out and balled up.

Mangy snapped his fingers and his comrades complied with his commands. Mark pulled the bandanna out of Tawny's mouth. He caught her off guard when he squeezed on her buttocks and shoved his tongue down her throat. She tried to fight him off, but he overpowered her and continued squeezing on her buttocks. Then he proceeded to squeeze her breasts. Mangy and Terror did nothing but laugh while everyone else looked on in horror. He started kissing on her neck and she continued trying to fight him off.

"Get off me. Stop it. Just stop it!" she cried in agony.

Mark grabbed her by her throat and quietly whispered in her ear, "If it wasn't for me having a prosthetic dick, I'd rape your old fine ass in front of everyone." Then he stuck his tongue in her ear and grinned wickedly.

You'd have thought Chucky the killer doll had reincarnated himself inside of him. Tawny burst into sobs while his hand was still around her throat.She cried in terror. Mark laughed again and kissed her on the cheek. Then he unlocked his fingers from around her neck and blew her a kiss. He looked down at Sylvester and spat on him. He, Mangy, and Terror all laughed in unison.

"Okay, pops! Show us the loot, and you'd better not be shitting us because your life depends on it," Mangy said in a chilling tone.

"Umm...umm, yes, sir. Um, pardon me, folks. I-I-I'll be right back," Pastor Milford said and the henchmen followed him into his office.

Tawny was shook up and leaned down before Sylvester. Sylvester moaned and laid there helplessly.

"I'll go and get you a towel, baby. I cannot believe those thugs did this to you," she said as she sniffled and cried. "I am so very sorry." She hung her head in shame.

"Sister, I'll go and get some towels, and then we'll take him to the emergency room," the groom volunteered and a few people from the crowd followed suit and consoled Tawny and Sylvester. Tawny couldn't have thought of anything more tragic than that day and she wouldn't have wished it on her worst enemy.

Sadly, Pastor Milford had to pay those gangsters every penny of the money that was secretly supposed to go toward buying himself a brand new BMW; the rest of it was supposed to be a down payment for Sylvester's dream house that he was going to surprise Tawny with. The pastor had announced to the church that he was going to use the money to buy another vehicle for the church, feed the homeless, and eradicate the mold that was forming on the ceilings of the men and women's restrooms. Due to the thugs throwing a monkey wrench in Pastor Milford's plans, and him being afraid of those gangsters returning, his attitude toward Sylvester became newer than a flat screen TV on Black Friday.

Sylvester was taken to the hospital and his hand was treated and bandaged. He lied and said that he accidentally stabbed himself while cutting a piece of fruit. However, before he could return back to the church, Pastor Milford had left a message on his voicemail telling him he could no longer return, and he was no longer welcome there. Sylvester and Tawny were devastated. Of course, the incident with the thugs permeated the small town like an outbreak. To save face, they moved away from the town they were in to start over brand new. Tawny and Sylvester vacated the small Virginian town, and relocated to Richmond, Virginia. They ended up moving into a small apartment together and they already knew if church folks knew about them living together, they'd have a field year by casting all sorts of stones at them.

Sylvester started his own landscaping business and he started ministering to the community. Strangely, the incident with the thugs solidified their bond and they ended up getting married a month later. Tawny was willing to forgive all of Sylvester's transgressions and work on a long-term future with him. Sylvester hadn't been in touch with his daughter Doreen, but Tawny really wanted the both of them to reconcile their differences. She prayed day and night for Doreen to have a change of heart. She believed that Sylvester was a changed man—or so she continued to tell herself.

The night before Pauline and Samuel had come to visit her and Sylvester, Tawny was shocked when she'd walked into their mini library room and caught Sylvester on his computer, masturbating while watching child pornography. He was so engrossed in his sick activity, he hadn't noticed she was watching him. He was breathing and panting ferociously and if that wasn't all, she witnessed him change the video to a blown up photo of a nude Doreen, who was posed with her legs spread wide open. Tawny continued to watch in horror as Sylvester licked his daughter's vagina through the screen.

Tawny hurriedly and silently left the room and covered her mouth in shame. She knew she couldn't confront Sylvester because she didn't know how to. "Oh. My. God. Lord, you gotta help us," Tawny cried out as she slid down against the wall and clutched the cross around her neck. Oh, Lord you gotta help us. That's my husband in that room. He's been possessed by Satan. Please rebuke that evil spirit, Lord, Tawny said silently.

Tawny never confronted Sylvester about her witnessing the depravity of his actions because she wanted to root herself in denial. She had no intentions of leaving him or telling Samuel and Pauline about what she'd seen .She promised to take it to her grave and pray the wickedness out of her husband so he'd become a better person. She swore to put on the Judy Cleaver façade that was really threatening to dismantle. How much longer did she think she could live a lie "in the name of Hay-zoos"?

~~ ~~

"Aw, honey. You really know how to make a woman feel appreciated," Pauline said and lightly bit on Samuel's ear while she laid her head on his well-chiseled chest.

"I do, don't I," Samuel replied with a confident smirk on his face and wrapped his burly strong arms around Pauline.

"Umm…hmm," Pauline replied.

"You wanna go for another round," Samuel asked.

Pauline chuckled. "Sure, I just need to go pee first and then we'll go for another session."

"Okay, beautiful. Don't keep me waiting too long, alright?" Samuel returned with a chuckle of his own.

"I won't, lover man," she said as she dressed. "I'll be back," she said and blew him a kiss.

He grabbed the air like he'd actually caught the kiss and rubbed his hand all over his body.

"You are so silly," she laughed as she stepped into the hallway.

Pauline entered the bathroom and shut the door. When she closed the door, the picture hanging on the wall fell face down on the floor. When she reached to pick it up, she saw that another smaller picture was taped to the back of it. She turned the picture over and it read: "Matthew 5:28: But I say to you that everyone who looks at a woman with lustful intent has already committed adultery with her in his heart." Pauline furrowed her brows and felt an eerie feeling in the pit of her stomach. The front of the smaller picture was facing the back of the bigger picture and she could tell it was taped to the back of it because she heard the slight plastic, crunching sound of the Scotch tape that was holding it together when she pressed it. As she peeled the little picture all the way back, she cupped her mouth in shock—the picture was of a little girl performing oral sex on a guy. She didn't want to believe that what she was seeing was Sylvester receiving oral sex by his own daughter.

As she felt the bile propelling its way up her esophagus, Pauline immediately lifted the toilet top and heaved. Once she was done, she struggled to inhale and exhale. She quickly washed her hands and face, grabbed the small picture without looking at it and placed it back onto the larger picture. She gently opened the door and glanced up and down the hallway to make sure no one was around. Then she quickly retreated back into the bedroom, sat on the bed and started rocking back and forth after laying the picture next to her.

"What's the matter, sweetheart?" Sylvester worriedly asked. "Are you alright? What's the matter?" he repeated when she failed to respond.

Pauline didn't say anything. She continued rocking back and forth. Samuel lifted himself up and searched the floor for his pants and shirt. When he found them, he put them on and he sat next to Pauline. He noticed the picture that she'd placed facedown next to her. He picked it up, turned it over and read the scripture.

"Look at the picture on the back of it," Pauline said in a quivering voice.

Samuel gave her a peculiar look and he did as she instructed. When he unpeeled the picture and saw the graphic content, he dropped it like it was a viper snake that had bitten him. "What the hell is that and where did you get it from? That better not be what I think it is," he said.

Pauline burst into tears and wrapped her arms around his neck. "I'm so-sorry. I'm very sorry," she said in between sniffles.

Samuel gave her another befuddled look like she had died five times and came back to life. "What...what are you talking about, Pauline? Listen, whatever it is you need to tell me, we'll work through this, okay?" he said. He tipped her chin up with his index finger so he could look into her eyes and gave her a reassuring look.

Pauline removed his finger from her chin and returned his gaze with a haunting and piercing stare. "Baby, it's not about me. It's about Sylvester. You were right. That man hasn't changed. I...I—"

"Shhhh...say no more." Samuel silenced her by putting his index finger over her lips and embraced her tightly. "I don't want you stressing yourself out over it. I'll take care of it. I want you to relax, alright?"

Pauline lifted her head and gave him a worried look. "W-w-wait, what are you going to do?" Pauline incredulously asked as more tears welled up in her eyes and cascaded down her flushed cheeks.

Samuel knew how paranoid Pauline could be when she was experiencing hysteria. "I'm going to speak to him," Samuel calmly said. Pauline gave him another look like she knew what he was about to do. "Honey, I promise I won't do anything crazy, okay? I'm only going to speak to him man-to-man," Samuel assured her and kissed her on her forehead. "I want you to get some rest."

Pauline did what she was told. She looked like she'd aged ten additional years within the last five minutes. She looked so frail and ashen that Samuel looked at her with pity in his eyes.

"I'll bring you a bottle of water when I return, okay?" he calmly told her.

She replied with a nod.

Samuel carefully exited the bedroom. Once he was in the hallway, he looked both ways to make sure Tawny wasn't around and descended the staircase. The last thing he wanted her to do was ask him questions. Let alone find out about her two-bit pedophile of a husband. Although he was sadly mistaken to assume she wasn't already aware. All of a sudden, he heard hard breathing and panting coming from the room adjacent to the dining room. He furrowed his eyebrows and followed the panting sound. As he got closer to the panting, chills slid down his spine like ice water. Samuel wanted to believe he was losing his mind, but reality wasn't having it any other way. By the he time reached the room, he saw the door had been left ajar. He quietly entered.

When he witnessed Sylvester rub his penis against the computer screen that displayed a picture of his own daughter Doreen, Samuel completely lost it; he charged at Sylvester and leaped on him like a Jaguar.

"You sick son of a bitch!" Samuel yelled and gave Sylvester a punch to his chin that lifted him out of his chair and slammed him into the bookshelf behind him; all of the books fell on him. Samuel vehemently yanked Sylvester by his ankles, dragged him from under the books and proceeded to repeatedly punch him in his face.

It wasn't long before Tawny heard the commotion and intervened. "Oh, sweet Jesus!" She tried to pull Samuel off Sylvester but he wouldn't budge. "Stop it, Samuel. You're killing him! Stop it!" she cried out and desperately tried to pry Samuel off her husband, but he wouldn't relent. "Take your hands off my husband or I'm calling the police," she frantically threatened.

Samuel finally ceased punching Sylvester. Sylvester's face was bloodied and mangled. He was out cold.

"Oh my God!" Tawny bent down to aid him.

Samuel looked at his fist, which was bloody, then he redirected his attention to Tawny and her pathetic husband. He really wanted to kill Sylvester.

"Why did you do this to my husband?" Tawny lashed out at him with tears streaming down her face.

Samuel was breathing hard but he remained calm. "I caught your perverted husband rubbing his penis against the computer screen that was displaying a naked picture of his own daughter," he said and clenched his hands. Samuel wanted to beat the wind out of Sylvester, but lucky for Sylvester, Tawny wasn't having it.

"I'm not going to sit here and listen to you malign my husband. He would never do such a thing. You and Pauline need to leave!" Tawny shot back.

Did this woman say what I thought she said? Samuel could have sworn he'd heard her deny her husband's depraved behavior. Samuel sighed and shook his head. "So, you're accusing me of lying on your sick ass husband? Why don't you look at the computer screen for yourself," he said with anger so fierce, it could have suffocated all three of them that very moment.

Tawny stood up and gave him a look that would have scared the freckles off Chucky the Killer Doll. "You watch your mouth, young man," she said while poking at his chest with her index finger. "My husband would do no such thing. And even if he did, what business of yours is it? Who the hell are you to come inside of another person's house and beat them senseless? You have your nerve!" Tawny barked while shaking her fist at Samuel. Poor Samuel was shocked. "Just look at him," she continued and pointed at the damage Samuel had inflicted upon her husband's face. "How could you, Samuel? And I thought you were a man of God!" she wailed and knelt down to touch Sylvester, who was moaning like a mad dog who'd been gunned down by his owner.

"You've got to be kidding me. You're going to defend this freak after what I told you, and then you're going to act like it's all my fault and he's the one who isn't in the wrong? I caught this bastard put—"

"I said that's enough!" Tawny yelled in a tone in that was so unfamiliar to Samuel, he flinched a little. Then she was overcome with an eerie calmness that creeped Samuel out. But what she said next alarmed him a hundred times more. "I'm aware that my husband is a pedophile who craves having sex with his own daughter at times, but it's nothing that you nor I can fix. Only our Lord and Savior can."

Samuel's mouth dropped so low, his tongue dried out within nanoseconds. "Mom, are you—"

"Shhh," Tawny calmly said. "I have vowed to be with my husband through sickness and health, richer or poorer until death do us part. I would never leave him just because he has a little mental sickness. It is a woman's duty to stick by her husband despite his short comings and transgressions. You, of all people, should know that, Samuel. My husband doesn't need counseling or jail time. Jesus was able to turn water into wine, therefore he can deliver my husband from his sickness too."

"Mom, please lis—"

"I don't wanna hear another word! It would be in the best interest of you and my ungrateful daughter to find a hotel room during the remainder of your stay in town. Both of you have disrespected me and my husband long enough. I'd appreciate it if you left now."

Samuel just put his hand on his head in a frustrated gesture. "This is preposterous! You mean to tell me that you're going to condone what this man has done to his own daughter?" he finally asked.

"I want you and my daughter out of my house within an hour or I'm calling the police," Tawny replied in an incensed but calm voice.

Samuel was seething and he was starting to see Tawny in the same light as her husband, because she was cavalier about everything he did. Samuel felt she might as well have been there watching Sylvester rape and molest his own daughter, and no telling how many other young girls. He was determined to say a few more words to her before he left. "You should call the police on yourself and your husband because you're both sick. And as for my daughter, Chastity, and the other baby that Pauline and I are about to have, you and your piss-poor ass excuse for a husband are no longer welcome to see them."

"God will punish you for that," Tawny said in a sinister tone.

This fucking bitch is pushing her luck! If I could get away with it, I would send her and her bitch ass husband to their maker faster than they could scratch their own asses from the burning of the flames they'll both endure in hell! Samuel thought but he left her with a thought to dwell on.

"You, and Sylvester the child molester have dug a grave for yourselves in hell," he said and walked out.